Nine Days
QUEEN

Karleen Bradford

Cover by Laurie McGaw

Scholastic-TAB Publications Ltd.
123 Newkirk Road, Richmond Hill, Ontario
Canada

I would like to express my appreciation to the Canada Council for the grant which enabled me to do the necessary research for this book in England.

Karleen Bradford

Canadian Cataloguing in Publication Data

Bradford, Karleen
  The nine days queen

ISBN 0-590-71617-4

1. Grey, Jane, Lady, 1537 1554 Juvenile fiction
I. Title

PS8553.R32N55 1986   jC813'.54   C86-093762-3
PZ7.B72Ni 1986

1st printing 1986   **Printed in Canada**

Manufactured by Webcom Limited

For Jane, herself

Contents

1. A summons from London 3
2. The boy king 18
3. A royal marriage? 32
4. Uneasy beginnings 43
5. Clouds gather 56
6. "You will pay for this, Uncle!" 71
7. Treason 86
8. Ill-fated betrothal 101
9. Forebodings 116
10. "Forgive me" 131
11. Queen Jane 144
12. The trap behind the crown 157
13. A time to be born 169
14. . . . And a time to die 183

The Tower
of London
February 12, 1554

The upstairs window of the narrow house on Tower Green was small and the glass of poor quality, giving a wavy picture of the view beyond. Nevertheless, Jane could see the scaffold that had been erected on the Green very clearly. It was draped in black cloth, and in the centre of it, surrounded by straw, was the stone that would serve as the executioner's block. There were four steps leading up to it.

In less than two hours, just weeks after her sixteenth birthday, Jane would be walking up those steps, kneeling, and laying her head on that block, her neck bare to the executioner's axe — guilty of treason in the highest measure against her grace, Queen Mary. Seven months ago it had been Jane who was queen: Queen Jane of England. But only for nine days.

And before that?

Before that she had been Lady Jane Grey, a child, content and secure at Bradgate Park, with a small tower room of her own filled with books, and time to write, and deer to walk amongst and pet in the rolling, forested park that surrounded the Manor House.

It seemed so long ago . . .

1
A summons from London

It was cold, even for February, and Jane drew her heavy woollen cloak more tightly around her, wishing she had bothered to take time to put on the warmer, fur-lined one. The wind was especially biting here at the top of the hill. The rest of the family would think her senseless to come up here on such a day, but it was Jane's favourite spot in all of Bradgate Park, no matter what the weather. From here she could look around on all sides and see the forests undulating away from her in waves that stretched to the full circle of the horizon. Up here she could be alone and free — something she craved, but that just wasn't possible back at the Manor House.

As she braced herself against the wind, one of the older stags came out of the forest onto the path and sniffed the air cautiously, then lowered his great, antlered head and began to search for food. There was a pile of browsewood near him — the small oak twigs the gamekeepers put out to sustain the deer through the winter — and Jane watched idly to see how long it would take him to find it.

Suddenly a movement on the road caught her eye. A horseman was coming from the direction of London. Jane stood up immediately. Her father was in London; he had gone there for old King Henry's funeral. They had had no word from him since he had left. Could this be a messenger from him?

Jane caught up the pony's reins, pulled her over to one of the jagged rocks that thrust itself so curiously out of the hillside, and climbed up on it quickly. It was a nuisance having to find something to climb up on every time she wanted to mount, but at nine years old there was no help for it. And she was particularly small for nine at that. She looked forward eagerly to the day when she would start growing a bit more quickly.

Jane raced the pony back to the Manor as speedily as possible. She galloped into the cobbled courtyard, threw her reins to the waiting groom, and ran straight for the winter parlour. She expected to find her mother sitting before the fire, but only Katherine, her younger sister, was there.

"Wherever have you been, Jane?" Katherine burst out as soon as she saw her. "Our lady mother is very annoyed with you. She has been waiting for you to attend her for supper these past twenty minutes."

Jane's heart sank. She hadn't realized how late it was. Her mother, always quick to anger even at the best of times, particularly disliked being kept waiting for her meals. Jane ran for the

4

stairs up to her little tower room. Her nurse, Mrs. Ellen, was waiting for her.

"Wherever have you been, my lady?" she asked, echoing Katherine. Her brows were drawn together in a worried frown. "Lady Frances will be furious. You know she hates to be kept waiting." Mrs. Ellen splashed cold water from a ewer on the table in the corner of the room into a basin as she spoke. "I do wish you wouldn't always be riding off by yourself, my lady. It's not seemly, really it isn't. I can't understand why you wish to," she fussed on. "It's not natural, wanting to be all by yourself like that."

Jane threw her cloak carelessly onto the bed and began to wash herself quickly, ignoring her old nurse's familiar fretting. "Did you see the messenger?" she asked. "Was he from London? Did he bring news of my lord father?" She wriggled impatiently as the woman hurriedly tried to tidy her and straighten her hair.

"I don't know anything about any messenger," Mrs. Ellen replied brusquely. "But I do know that if you're not down to attend upon your lady mother immediately, you'll be in for a whipping and bed without your supper."

In her haste she pulled Jane's hair. Jane winced, but didn't complain. She knew Mrs. Ellen spoke the truth. With a last pat, Mrs. Ellen pushed her out of the room.

Jane ran back down the stairs and into the small, private dining room where she and her mother dined when her father was away. Katherine and Mary, the baby of the family, dined with their nurses upstairs, but Jane was old enough

5

now to take up her duty of attending upon her mother.

She dashed into the room just as her mother swept in from the front parlour, accompanied by three other ladies and the family chaplain, Dr. Haddon. Jane composed herself quickly, curtsied as they took their seats, then hurried to stand behind Lady Frances.

"Good even, my lady mother," she said, trying not to puff.

Her mother answered her with a glare, and motioned to the servants to bring on the first course as soon as the grace had been spoken.

Jane was full of impatience to hear what news the courier had brought, but knew better than to speak as she handed her mother the Lady Frances's own special set of knives. She was grateful that her lateness had only merited a glare, not a cuff on the ear or worse.

The Lady Frances Grey, Jane's mother, was as large as Jane was tiny. Her broad, red-cheeked face bore a startling and somewhat unfortunate resemblance to her uncle, the well-beloved old King Henry, whose death just the month before had so shocked and saddened all of England. As well as her looks she had, even more unfortunately, inherited a good measure of the king's famed ill temper, but without the sense of humour that redeemed it.

Throughout the long, interminable meal Jane stood silently, not daring to voice the questions in her mind, handing her mother the dishes as the servants brought them in and passing them back when Lady Frances had finished with them. By the time the first washing of hands had been accomplished and the subtleties and other sweets brought in, she was shifting from foot to foot and chafing at the ritual. When she finally handed her mother the moist towel for the final washing, she couldn't quite cover the sigh of relief that escaped her. Her mother glared at her again with annoyance, then rose and signalled the others to follow her to the warmth of the winter parlour for a last cup of hot, mulled wine.

Now it was Jane's own turn to eat, but she made very quick work of the many courses of soups, meats, and fish. For once her parents' strict instructions only to choose one or two samples from each course were easy to follow. She even hurried through the comfit, wanting only to finish and join her mother.

As soon as she entered the winter parlour, she knew that something unusual was indeed afoot. Katherine had been summoned down from the nursery and was standing meekly in front of the fire. She gave Jane a quick, questioning glance from across the room, but Jane signalled back with a slight shrug of the shoulders. She didn't know any more than Katherine did about what was going on.

Their mother looked at them, disapprovingly as usual, and cleared her throat to speak. The other ladies busied themselves in a corner of the room with their embroidery.

"I have had word from my lord, your father," Lady Frances began. "Stand up straighter, Jane. It's bad for the health to slouch so after eating." She paused for a moment while Jane stiffened her spine and clasped her hands tightly together in front of her, then she continued. "You both know that your father was given the honour of being chief mourner at his grace, King Henry's funeral, may God have mercy on his soul. It seems that King Edward now, in his wisdom, has decided to carry on with the honours bestowed upon us by his royal father. My lord, your father, has been appointed Lord High Constable for the young king's coronation, and so will carry the sword of state before him. He has been invested with the Order of the Garter for the occasion."

Jane and Katherine looked at each other again. This was a very great honour to come to their house, notwithstanding the fact that King Edward was their cousin.

"Your lord father wishes me to join him in London as soon as possible so that I may be there for the coronation and the festivities pertaining to it. I shall take you both with me."

At this news both girls broke into wide smiles. London! They hadn't been to their London house for almost a year!

"We shall have to pack with the utmost haste, however, if we are to reach London in time," Lady Frances continued, still glowering at them. "The coronation is a little less than two weeks away, and it will take most of that time to get there. Your nurses will begin packing your things tomorrow; we will leave as soon as possible. Your lord father has Dorset House waiting in readiness for us."

Jane and Katherine curtsied and made as if to leave. They were bursting with excitement at the news and could hardly wait to get up to the privacy of their rooms to discuss it. Lady Frances put out a restraining hand, however.

"There is one thing more. Jane, do you remember when her grace, Queen Katherine, visited with us last summer?" She spoke again before Jane could answer. "At that time we discussed sending you to her household to be brought up properly in the ways of a lady at court, but with the illness of his grace, King Henry, it was not possible. Now, however, she has sent word that you are to come to her at Chelsea Palace after the coronation. The Princess Elizabeth is with her as well. You will take your place with them as a member of the royal family." With a wave of her hand, Lady Frances finally dismissed her daughters.

Jane and Katherine curtsied yet again and left the room demurely. When they reached the broad, carved, oaken staircase, however, they broke into a delighted run and raced each other up. At the top, in the passageway outside her own tower room, Jane struggled to control herself. Katherine was two years younger than she — it was acceptable for her to behave in such a wanton manner. But she was almost grown and going to live with the queen!

"Jane! Can you believe it? To live with Queen Katherine and the Princess Elizabeth at court! Isn't it exciting? How can you bear it?"

Katherine's cheeks were flushed and her eyes sparkling. Even at seven she was the acknowledged beauty of the family. Jane looked at her and for a moment felt a pang of envy. How much more beautiful Katherine would look amongst all the fine ladies at court than would she. Katherine's hair was dark and lustrous, Jane's light and sandy, almost red. It was the Tudor inheritance from her famous great-uncle, King Henry, she knew, and she shared it with both the new King Edward and his sister, Princess Elizabeth, but still she hated it. And worst of all, she had freckles. Possibly the worst blemish a young girl could have. No matter how many times she rubbed them with elder water, they still stood out stubbornly across her small, tip-tilted nose, even in the dead of winter when the sun hadn't shone for weeks. Jane shook her head. There was nothing to be done about it. And it *was* she, not Katherine, who was going to court.

"Aren't you excited?" Katherine repeated, tugging at her older sister's sleeve impatiently.

"Of course I am," Jane answered. "But think how we must hurry and get prepared. Our lady mother will not tolerate it if we are not ready to leave when she is." Then, in spite of herself, her own eyes began to sparkle and she grabbed Katherine's hands and swung her around in a wild dance. "London, Katherine! We're going to London! And we'll see King Edward! Do you think he'll remember me, Katherine? It is over a year since we last met. Do you think he'll remember a cousin who is exactly the same age he is?"

Mrs. Ellen popped her head out of Jane's room and reached out to haul her in, just as Katherine's nurse came puffing up the stairs to retrieve her. Trailing behind her, unable to manage the stairs too well, laboured Mary, the smallest sister of the three. Jane saw her and broke away from Mrs. Ellen. She ran to pick her up and hold her close. Small as Jane was, Mary was even smaller, almost dwarfish. Perhaps because of this she held a special place in Jane's heart.

Mary looked up at Jane questioningly, obviously wondering what all the excitement was about.

"I'm going to London," Jane cried. Then she sobered up immediately as she saw the tiny face pinch with disappointment. "Not for long, baby," she said, cuddling her close. "Not for long." But even as she reassured her, Jane felt an odd lurch in her heart. Suddenly all the excitement faded.

How long would she be gone? From Mary. From Bradgate. From everything she had known and loved all her life. How long *would* she be gone?

*   *   *

The next few days were occupied with getting clothes ready and packed for the journey to London. Lessons, which usually occupied most of Jane's and Katherine's days, were put aside almost completely. Katherine was only too delighted by this, but Jane missed them. She missed the orderliness of her usual life, too. And in the midst of all her eager expectations, there were many questions and worries nagging at her. What would life be like in London at Queen Katherine's palace? How would she get along with the Princess Elizabeth?

11

Her mother was very definite in telling her that she was not to be intimidated. "Your breeding and lineage are royal too," Lady Frances reminded her more than once. "Remember that my mother was old King Henry's youngest sister. And *you* have never been declared a bastard," she added with a sniff. She was referring to the fact that Elizabeth, along with her older sister Mary, had been declared illegitimate by King Henry, even though they were his daughters.

It was done only to suit the king's own purposes, Jane thought with a certain amount of contempt. He had his marriage to Mary's mother, the Spanish princess Catherine of Aragon, annulled because he wanted to marry Anne Boleyn, Elizabeth's mother. Then he had Anne Boleyn executed because of suspected unfaithfulness so that he could marry Jane Seymour, Edward's mother. Indeed, he even hinted he doubted that Anne's child, Elizabeth, was his daughter — although anyone who saw the flaming red hair and the Tudor pride of the princess could never seriously believe otherwise.

When Jane Seymour, Edward's mother, died in childbirth, King Henry took three other wives in quick succession. Anne of Cleves was also put aside (this time because she was ugly and smelled, it was rumoured); poor Catherine Howard suffered the same fate as Anne Boleyn — accused of unfaithfulness and treason and sent to the block; but Queen Katherine Parr, his last wife, cleverly managed to keep her head on long enough to outlive him.

These thoughts raced through Jane's mind, but she certainly didn't speak them aloud to her mother. Even to think them was tantamount to treason. Besides, while Lady Frances might refer to the Princess Elizabeth as a bastard, she would hear no such thing of the Princess Mary. Although she, along with the rest of the Grey family, had followed the reformation of the old religion during King Henry's reign and was now a Protestant, she did not approve of the annullment of his marriage with the first Queen Catherine. To her, the Princess Mary was the first and only true daughter of King Henry. In fact, Mary was a valued and treasured friend of Lady Frances Grey, even though she still clung to the old Catholic religion.

But Jane was not likely to have much to do with the Princess Mary. It was the Princess Elizabeth with whom she would be living, and that princess was rumoured to have a temper as flaming as the colour of her hair. Despite her mother's proud words, that thought kept intruding uneasily into Jane's excited anticipation.

There wasn't too much time for worrying, however. Within a week everything was ready. The assemblage that was to leave for London was a large one. They would go by horseback, of course, stopping at inns or the manor houses of friends and relatives at night. Besides Jane, Katherine and Lady Frances, there would be a whole retinue of footmen, nurses, servants, and assorted relatives who had decided to come along. There would also be a large number of horses and

13

mules carrying all the baggage that was accompanying them. It was a major accomplishment, getting everything organized, and when they set out, only two hours later than they had originally intended, on another wet, windy February morning, it looked as if a ragged army were in full march.

Jane pulled her cloak tightly around her — the fur-lined one this time — and drew the hood closely around her face. The horses' breath steamed in the cold morning air. As they began to move, the treacherous clay sucked at the animals' hooves and threatened to mire them with every step they took. Jane looked back once, then turned her face resolutely forward.

At noontime they stopped and ate a picnic that the servants spread out on rugs in a sheltered grove of trees. Jane was glad of the chance to rest, but Katherine darted over as soon as she dismounted. "Isn't it wonderful, Jane?" she burbled. It seemed that no weather, no matter how wet and uncomfortable, could dampen her enthusiasm.

By evening, however, when they stopped at a small inn, even Katherine was tired. Several of the servants had ridden ahead of the main party to alert the innkeepers of their prospective guests, so there were fires lit and meat roasting on spits by the time they arrived. The warmth and excited bustle that greeted them was very welcome.

After they had eaten, Jane lay in the bed she shared with Katherine and tried to think of Bradgate and of the sister she had left behind, but almost immediately her thoughts turned ahead. Already her old life seemed to have receded far into the past, and London, with its glittering enticements, hovered just beyond the horizon.

The journey took almost seven days, and was conducted at a strenuous pace. Lady Frances was in her element — there was nothing she liked better than riding, whether to the hunt or on a trip such as this. Jane and Katherine were hard put to keep up, but Lady Frances made no allowances for them, or for the terrible condition of the roads. The condition of their lodgings, too, was not always as pleasant as on the first night. Cold food and a straw pallet in a drafty anteroom were all they enjoyed some nights. By the time they reached the outskirts of London City itself, even Katherine was exhausted.

When the spires and steeples of the city began to rise into view, however, the spirits of both girls began to rise with them. Just a few hours more and they would be in Dorset House, their London home, where fires would be burning, steaming hot food set out, and best of all, soft beds plumped and warmed and waiting for them.

As they rode into the city, their progress slowed. Jane had forgotten just how crowded, noisy, and dirty it was. People milled about, jostling each other and crying out greetings or oaths; vendors hawked their wares at the tops of their voices; dogs barked and snapped at the horses' heels. The servants on foot went before them in the narrow streets, trying to clear a path, but even so, they could only pick their way through the throngs at a snail's pace. There was filth and confusion everywhere.

By the time they finally reached Dorset House, Jane was feeling sick and faint. The sight of it, however, and the knowledge that their journey was over at last, made her take heart.

Her father, alerted by the servants who had gone on ahead, was standing on the broad stone steps waiting for them. As she caught sight of his slim, elegantly clad figure, Jane checked quickly to see what kind of mood he was in. He seemed relaxed, and his fine-featured, almost too handsome face was smiling. Jane let out the breath she had been holding. Although to the rest of the world the Marquis of Dorset seemed an amiable, affable, easy-going man, his children knew only too well the dark side of his temper. Both Jane and Katherine had felt the strength behind the hand that now rested so lightly and casually on his sword hilt.

"Welcome!" he cried, as he moved forward to help Lady Frances dismount. "You are well come indeed, and have made good time on your journey."

Lady Frances smiled and preened herself. "We have, my lord. I have spared no effort to bring us to you as hastily as possible."

"And just in time, my lady wife," Lord Dorset answered. "Preparations for the coronation are going on apace. It's well you've arrived in such good time."

Jane accepted the hand of the groom who leaped forward to assist her. Within minutes she was sitting in front of a roaring fire, Mrs. Ellen had removed her muddy riding cloak, and a serving girl had handed her a cup of hot, mulled wine. Jane sipped it gratefully.

Gradually the dank chill that seemed to have penetrated right into her bones began to give way to a comforting warmth. Her father was describing the forthcoming events, and she leaned forward eagerly to hear him. A sense of anticipation was fast rising within her. Now that she was actually here, ensconced in the familiar luxury of Dorset House, all her earlier doubts and worries seemed ridiculous. A whole new chapter of her life was opening up before her, full of excitement and enticing possibilities. Now she was avid to get on with it.

2
The boy king

The royal procession from the Tower of London —
where the kings of England always stayed while
awaiting their coronations — to Westminster
Palace was to take place in three days. The actual
coronation ceremony would be the day after that.
Those three days were filled with a bustle and
preparations that made the previous bustle and
preparations for leaving Bradgate Manor seem
small. When the gowns were unpacked, shaken
out, and hung up to air, it was found that Jane's
best kirtle, which she hadn't worn for over a year,
was too short and too tight in the bodice.

"When I wish to grow I don't," she wailed,
"but when I don't wish to, I do!" She turned back
and forth in front of the wavy mirror in the bed-
room she shared with Katherine, frantically
trying to do up buttons that just wouldn't meet.

"Hush now and don't fret," Mrs. Ellen reassured her. She was already fumbling for needle
and thread. "I knew when I made that last year
that you'd be growing, and there's a goodly
amount of material to let out. If you'll just stand
still for a moment, I'll measure it for you. Stand
still, my lady, for mercy's sake!"

Katherine had no such problems. Jane watched with envy as she twirled, the skirts of her pale yellow silk tabby kirtle swirling and rustling around her. The colour suited her well, and her cheeks were flushed with excitement. It was impossible to be jealous of her, however. There was too much fun and good humour shining out of her eyes.

"Will we have good seats for viewing the procession, do you think, Jane?" she asked anxiously. "Will we see everything?"

Jane laughed. "Our lord father has made certain of that! He has places reserved for all of us near to Westminster Palace itself. We'll see everything there is to be seen, do not doubt it."

"I wish we could go to the coronation as well, Jane. Wouldn't that be grand?"

"Well, we can't, my little goose, but you can be certain our lady mother will tell us all about it."

The two girls giggled. They knew well that the Lady Frances would be talking of nothing else for weeks to come.

They wouldn't be attending the banquet afterwards either, but much to Jane's delight, her father had told her she would be allowed to go to the masque at the palace that evening, and to watch the jousts and tournaments the next day. It would be her parents' chance to present her to the new king and to renew her acquaintance with Queen Katherine.

*   *   *

Jane awoke early on the morning of the royal

procession. She fought her way impatiently out of the enormous, pillowy, four-poster bed, tossing aside the heavy coverings. The chill in the room struck her as soon as she poked her nose out through the bed-curtains, but she barely paused. What was the weather like? It had been raining for most of the time since they had arrived, and procession or no procession, she had no wish to sit all day on hard board stands in the drizzle. To her relief, the cobbled courtyard outside was dry. The sky was grey and lowering, but with luck, it wouldn't rain.

"Wake up, Katherine, you lazy lie-abed!" she cried, and ran back to pounce on her sister.

Katherine's face appeared above the covers immediately. "Is it fine?" she asked.

"Welladay, it's not raining," Jane answered. "That's good enough."

There was a light tap on the door. Mrs. Ellen bustled in, calling instructions to the two serving girls who followed her. Within minutes the fire had been replenished and Katherine's nurse had joined them, and they began the business of dressing. Another servant brought warm ale and saffron buns for Jane and Katherine to nibble on; there would be no time for anything else before they left.

Finally they were ready. Mrs. Ellen hurried them along to their mother's room, just in time to see Lady Frances sweep majestically out, her large, stout body encased in green velvet and adorned with pearls, rubies, and gold. Her face was heavily powdered, her small mouth pursed in its usual set of annoyed disdain. Her little piggy eyes passed over her two daughters without really seeing them as she addressed a footman beyond.

"Are the horses ready and waiting? We must leave at once."

"Yes, my lady," was the timorous answer.

Lady Frances launched herself down the staircase, leaving Jane and Katherine to bob along behind in her wake. A full retinue of footmen accompanied them to their reserved places — sorely needed, since the conduits had been running with wine and beer since daybreak and a goodly part of the crowd through which they pushed their way was already drunk. Mrs. Ellen wrinkled her nose disdainfully at the rioting, roaring masses. Even Katherine was momentarily daunted as one young man, clad in the traditional blue apprentice gown, grabbed at her stirrup and made her an elaborate bow. Jane, however, was too busy looking around her to worry.

London had been transformed. Banners and pennants hung from every house and balcony. Garlands of greenery were draped over doorways. Cloth of gold arras dripped over the grey and white buildings and the black woodwork, creating its own brilliant sunshine against the steely winter sky. At almost every corner or church a masque or fantasy had been set up. At St. George's Church a line had been strung from the steeple to the ground, and a man poised there ready to perform acrobatics and slide down the line headfirst when the king passed by. Jane learned afterwards that the king's grace had been so entranced by his performance that he had tarried there and held up the procession for fifteen minutes, watching and congratulating him!

The people all around them were shouting, carousing, and singing lustily. One refrain in particular Jane heard constantly:

Sing up heart, sing up heart,
And sing no more down,
For joy of King Edward
That weareth the crown.

She even found herself humming it as her pony picked her way over the freshly-gravelled streets.

At last they arrived at the spot where seats had been reserved for them. The tipstaffs who were guarding the seats and keeping the crowds back bowed to them, then helped them off their horses.

"The highest ones, Jane!" Katherine cried, scrambling for the very top row of the rough planks that had been set up. "We must sit up there so we can see it all!"

Jane found herself scrambling up after her just as eagerly. It was difficult to remain dignified amidst this chaotic frenzy.

It was hours before the procession was due to pass here, but there was so much to see and comment on that the time passed quickly. Aldermen, craftsmen, clerks of the city, and their families crowded the street. Priests were much in evidence — the elegantly black-robed Catholic priests just as much as their more simply garbed Protestant counterparts. From somewhere just out of sight came the sound of a full choir

22

rehearsing. Hunger was no problem, as there was a constant stream of vendors offering tansy cakes, sweetmeats, meat pies, and a host of other tidbits to munch on, and earthenware goblets of beer and wine with which to wash them down. Finally, though, a swelling murmur swept through the crowd.

"They're coming! They're coming!"

Katherine bounced up so impetuously that Jane grabbed at her to keep her from falling. Then they could hear the clear call of trumpets ringing out.

The first figures to be seen were the tall, armoured horsemen clattering past, resplendent in their surcoats of blue, purple, scarlet, and green. The nobles of the realm followed — courtiers, clergy, statesmen, and foreign ambassadors — hundreds of riders and men on foot. Jane waited in a fever of impatience for her first glimpse of the boy king — her cousin Edward. There was a small gap in the procession, then she saw her father. He was riding immediately before the king, carrying the sword of state. The Order of the Garter glittered on his breast. Jane had never seen him looking so impressive nor so magnificent. But her eyes were drawn to the knot of noblemen who followed him, and to the boy who rode so confidently in front of them.

Edward sat his horse with ease and dignity, holding himself imperiously erect. He was dressed in a gown of silver cloth, embroidered in gold and flashing with rubies and diamonds. His doublet and the soft buskins on his feet were also encrusted with jewels and pearls. On his head was a white velvet cap, so thickly set with diamonds and pearls as to make a dazzling halo. The whole glittering white and gold figure, mounted on a horse caped in scarlet and gold, stood out against the rest of the procession.

Beside Edward, providing a startling contrast, rode a tall, bearded man gowned in black with a small white ruff around his neck. A circlet of diamonds sparkling beneath the brim of his wide, low, black hat was all that brightened his appearance. His face was stern, and even from where she stood Jane could see the furrows of worry on his brow.

"The Duke of Somerset," Mrs. Ellen breathed at her side. "The Protector. He'll take good care of our blessed young king."

Six more mounted noblemen carried the canopy over the king's head. One of them chanced to turn her way just as he passed Jane, and she was startled to see how young he was. He couldn't have been much older than Edward himself! He smiled and waved to the crowd as they rode by. Jane caught her breath as his eyes met hers directly and held them for a second. He was tall — much taller than Edward in the saddle. To Jane's surprise, she found that the memory of his face remained clearly etched in her mind long after he had passed by. It was not merely that he was handsome — although he certainly was that — but there was something in his look that had appealed to her immediately.

I wonder who he is, she found herself thinking. I wonder if I will meet him when I see Edward tomorrow.

"Jane! I've spoken to you twice. Can you not hear me?"

Katherine was jogging her elbow excitedly. Jane blushed as if her sister could actually read her thoughts, then turned her attention to her. The tumultuous noise of the crowds was such that she couldn't really make out much of what her sister was saying.

The procession concluded with several thousand men-at-arms, yeomen of the guard, halberdiers, and grooms of the Privy Council marching in sections. Katherine was all for staying until the very last one of them had gone by, but once the king had passed, the Lady Frances lost interest. With difficulty, they left their seats and pushed their way away from the street where the procession was still marching by, the girls reluctantly following the swath their mother cut through the crowd.

That night both Jane and Katherine were too dazzled to go to sleep right away. They lay curled up together in their bed, talking and reliving over and over the marvels of the day. Katherine finally succumbed and closed her eyes, but Jane lay for a long time more, staring into the darkness, remembering. Edward hadn't looked at all like the small, studious boy she remembered. He had looked like a king. Young as he was, he had looked like a king. Touched by God. Tomorrow he would be annointed by the priests in God's name, and he would be their king by God's holy will.

It was a terrifying thing! What would it be like to assume that sacred burden? To know that you were chosen by God to rule His people? A sense of awe and reverence filled her. No, Edward was not the same boy she remembered. He would never be that same boy again. He was the king now. *Her* king.

*   *   *

The next morning Jane was awakened by a hand shaking her shoulder violently.

"My lady! You are to go! Your lord father has just sent word. You are to go to the coronation! Get up, my lady. Get up!"

Jane roused herself sleepily, not able to make sense of the words. Mrs. Ellen's flushed face swam into view.

"Mrs. Ellen. What is it? What is the hour? Surely it is too early to be up?"

"You must, my lady. Your lord father has sent word that you may accompany your lady mother to the coronation. His grace, King Edward, specifically requested that you be there!"

This time the words sank in. "Me? Edward asked for me to go?"

"*King* Edward, my lady," Mrs. Ellen corrected her reprovingly. "Yes, my lady. The king's grace himself wishes you to attend his coronation. You must be ready within the hour!"

This morning there was no time at all to worry about food. Besides, Jane was far too excited. When one of the serving maids brought a glass of ale, she waved the girl away impatiently. In one hour exactly, she was ready and waiting upon her mother.

Today they rode straight to Westminster

Abbey. The crowds around were immense, and if anything, there was more noise and celebration than the day before. Inside, all was colour and confusion. The majestic, pillared, grey stone arches of the abbey were hung with banners; the choir was resplendent with hangings of cloth of gold arras. The smooth paving stones underfoot had been covered with fresh rushes — the scent of crushed herbs rose from them and masked somewhat the more pervasive smell of packed, perspiring humanity.

Jane could recognize no one in the crush around them, but her mother was in her element. Lady Frances turned first one way, then the other, greeting all around her by name as regally as if she were queen herself. Jane shrank onto the bench beside her, trying to make herself as unnoticeable as possible, while at the same time trying to look all around her. Suddenly, to her horror, she felt her mother grab her by the arm.

"My daughter, the Lady Jane," Lady Frances was beginning in a voice that seemed to Jane to carry throughout the whole length of the vaulted chapel, when mercifully the sound of trumpets announced the arrival of the king's procession.

The dean of Westminster Abbey walked in first, with the full choir behind him singing a hymn. Their soaring voices filled the vast abbey, echoing and re-echoing within the old stone walls with a clarity and beauty that was almost painful. Instantly the cathedral was alive. While Jane sat, shivering with the wonder of it, the ladies around her leaped to their feet, jostling and craning their necks to get a view of those now entering the abbey.

Edward was preceded by his uncle, the Duke of Somerset. As the king's Protector, the duke carried the crown. Next came the Duke of Suffolk, Jane's grandfather, carrying the orb. Jane's father followed the old Duke of Suffolk and carried the royal sceptre. Behind him walked Edward.

But Jane's eye was drawn to the man behind the king, who held his train. He was elegantly slim, dressed all in black velvet, and had black hair, moustache and — against the fashion of the time — a small, neatly-trimmed, pointed beard. His eyes flashed with a peculiar intensity as they took in every aspect of the abbey and all those within it. His mouth was set in a hard, calculating pout. Jane stared at him as he walked by. Never, she thought, had she ever seen such a cold face! Still, that could hardly explain the feeling of revulsion, amounting almost to fear, that suddenly swept over her.

"John Dudley," one of the ladies whispered to another. "The Earl of Warwick."

"And none too happy about his position in the procession, it would seem," whispered another slyly.

"Hush!" a shocked voice exclaimed. "It's said he is a man of vaulting ambition. It might be well not to criticize him."

Jane's attention was finally distracted from that disturbing figure by Edward himself. Today he was dressed in a surcoat, train, and gown of crimson velvet, embroidered in gold and richly furred. He looked almost lost in the elaborate robes, but still carried himself with the dignity and majesty of a king. He was followed by a group of young boys, obviously his friends and schoolfellows. Without realizing what she was doing, Jane searched amongst them for the tall boy she had noticed yesterday. When she picked him out, she relaxed unconsciously and smiled a little, completely forgetting the dark figure who had gone before him.

The dean and the choir walked on through the long, pillared passage of the abbey to the altar, where the Archbishop of Canterbury was standing — a dazzling figure himself in robes of white and gold. There they turned and all waited for Edward, who moved on alone to St. Edward the Confessor's Chair. As soon as he was seated, the Archbishop turned to the great concourse of people assembled there and began to speak.

"Sirs, here present is Edward, rightful and undoubted inheritor by the laws of God and man to the Crown . . ."

His voice rolled on. Jane found herself caught up in the beauty and majesty of the ancient ceremony. When the Archbishop finished speaking, without hesitation she joined her voice to cry with the others: "Yea! Yea! Yea! God save King Edward!"

Edward was then conducted to the high altar where the Archbishop was now kneeling. He prostrated himself face down on the floor before the Archbishop, while the music of the choir and organ swelled and rolled to a triumphant crescendo.

The ceremony went on. Jane was so involved she hardly noticed the passing of time at first, but gradually she tired. Because of Edward's youth, the ceremony had been shortened to only seven hours, instead of the usual eleven or twelve, but as the time passed, Jane began to feel faint. The lack of any food or drink was beginning to tell.

Finally, however, Edward returned to the Confessor's Chair, and the Archbishop approached him with the crown. Jane sat up straight again. This was the truly stirring, most important part of the whole ceremony. A hush descended on all the chattering ladies. Only the sonorous voice of the Archbishop and the triumphant echoes of the choir could be heard as Edward made his vows and the crown was placed upon his head. The marriage ring was placed on his finger; he was invested with the orb and sceptre. As the crowned King of England, Edward turned to receive the homage of his peers.

His uncle, the Duke of Somerset, the Lord Protector, was the first to kneel before him, kissing his right foot and then his cheek, while the Mass of the Holy Ghost was sung. One by one, the other peers of the realm followed.

The Archbishop then turned back to the congregation. He spoke in ringing tones that carried throughout the abbey. "You will now join me in a prayer for His Sacred and Royal Majesty, Edward VI, Defender of the Faith, King of England, Scotland, Ireland, and France."

They prayed. The Archbishop spoke the final blessing. As Edward prepared to leave, Jane was astonished to find tears coursing down her cheeks. She was not alone. Men and women alike wept unashamedly as they cheered the boy who walked out so bravely under the scarlet canopy of state.

"God save King Edward!" they cried.

"God's blessings on the king!"

"He's old Harry's son, all right," a wizened old man near Jane exclaimed gleefully. "Look at the way the young peacock struts. It's his father all over again!"

To Jane at that moment, her future, and indeed, the future of all England, had never looked brighter.

3

A royal marriage?

The banquet that followed the coronation went on for hours, until Jane almost began to wish she hadn't been invited to it after all. But at first it was exciting, even though she was seated amongst a gaggle of giggling girls and very minor ladies-in-waiting. Each course was brought into the great banqueting hall of Westminster Palace to the sound of trumpets, and to Jane's astonishment, preceded by two noblemen on horseback.

Jane was so hungry she forgot all manners completely and gorged herself on everything within reach. Manners did not seem to be too important at this feast, however. Haunches of venison, platters of wildfowl, elaborately presented fish — all disappeared as quickly as they appeared. The ladies around her were digging in just as enthusiastically as she was, and everyone's fingers were dripping grease.

After her hunger had been satisfied, Jane began to droop. The events of the past two days had been more exhausting than anything she had ever known. Meat pies, pigeons, whole roasted boars came and went, but she saw them only in a daze. Even the masque that followed the meal — a presentation of the story of Orpheus in the underworld — made little impression on her until one of the hundreds of lighted tapers on the stage toppled over onto a pile of paper flowers. The flames that immediately shot up added immeasurably to the underworld effect, Jane thought, but she was too tired to be very worried, even though her companions screamed and scrambled for safety. Fortunately a footman had the presence of mind to throw a flagon of wine onto the blaze, and the fire obligingly died. The masque then resumed, none the worse for the incident except for one wine-stained demon.

No sooner had the last words of the presentation been spoken than King Edward rose. He, too, was beginning to show signs of the weariness that was so heavy on Jane. He bowed to the assemblage.

"Thank you, good ladies and gentlemen. We are well pleased that you have assisted at our coronation and have shown such love and devotion to our person. We look forward to seeing you all again on the morrow." Then he left.

Jane stood up slowly, not certain what she should do. In the general milling around and confusion she had lost sight of Lady Frances, who earlier had been sitting with her grace, Queen Katherine. Suddenly a hand reached out and touched her arm.

"My lady? Will you follow me?" It was one of the footmen who had waited on the king's table.

Not quite certain what to expect, Jane made her way through the crowds behind him.

He led her behind the screens, to a narrow, circular stone staircase that wound its way upwards. Jane followed. At the top, he brushed aside a tapestry and held it back for Jane to go through. She found herself in a comfortable room where a fire burned brightly. On the hearth lay a small dog. Seated on a chair beside the fire, stockinged feet stretched out to enjoy its warmth and to tickle the dog's stomach, was a young boy. It took Jane a second to recognize her cousin.

"Your majesty!" she gasped, and sank into a deep curtsy.

"Rise, cousin! You were not so formal the last time we met!"

Jane looked up to see Edward's eyes twinkling at her. Now she remembered him. Now he looked more like the boy who had teased her about her freckles and pulled her hair.

"You were not king the last time we met!" The words were out of her mouth before she could stop them.

There was an audible gasp from the other side of the room. Only then did Jane realize they were not alone. A tall girl with unruly, flaming red hair stood beside one of the casement windows. The Princess Elizabeth!

Jane tried to stand up and curtsy again, all at the same time, and stumbled. It was all she could do not to tumble onto the floor. Elizabeth arched an eyebrow at her clumsiness.

"We have met once before, have we not, Lady Jane?" she said.

"Yes, your highness," Jane stuttered.

"Oh, Elizabeth, don't be such a prig," Edward

said impatiently. "You remember our cousin as well as I do. How did you like the coronation?" he asked eagerly, turning back to Jane. "Wasn't it splendid?"

"It was, your grace. Perfectly splendid. Thank you for sending for me." Jane's weariness began to vanish as she slowly recovered her poise. She rose from her curtsy and stood before Edward, smiling at him and, a little uncertainly, at Elizabeth.

"I wanted you to come. And I sent for you tonight because I couldn't wait to see you again. We did have some good times together, didn't we?"

"Yes, we did." Jane's face lit up. "Remember the time you pushed the footman into the reflecting pool?"

Edward laughed. "Well, milady, I didn't really mean to. He was in my way, and I couldn't let *you* win the race!"

"I did anyway, though, didn't I?"

"You did," Edward conceded reluctantly. "Do *you* remember the time you told poor silly Lady Brampton that the old cow that ambled up behind her when we were picnicking was a bull?"

Jane giggled, completely at ease with her cousin now, the presence of the Princess Elizabeth forgotten. "I've never seen anyone scramble over a fence stile so quickly. Have you?"

"Never before and never since."

Jane spent half an hour with Edward, and it was as if they had parted only days before, not months. Edward called for a page and had him pull out a stool for Jane to sit on beside him. In the flickering light of the fire, the two were remarkably alike. They had the same pale colouring, the same fine, delicate features. Both of them had now forgotten the Princess Elizabeth. It was with a start of surprise that Jane heard her speak.

"I think, my lord brother, that the Lady Jane should return to her parents now. They are waiting for her, I am sure."

"Oh, Jane, forgive me. It is very late and I've kept you far too long. Go now, and I'll see you tomorrow at the tournament." He held out his hand. Jane kissed it, bobbed a quick curtsy, and turned to go. Elizabeth's voice brought her up short.

"And were you so ill brought up in the country, milady, that you were not taught to do proper reverence to your king?"

Jane flushed and, her eyes riveted on the Turkish carpet at her feet, turned to drop a low, sweeping curtsy to Edward. She was burning with shame. How could she have forgotten? Her mother had lectured her over and over as to the proper procedure to follow when she first met Edward!

"With your leave, your grace, I will retire now as well." As if to shame Jane further, Elizabeth made no less than five reverential obeisances as she backed away from Edward towards the door.

Jane remained frozen in her curtsy until she left. Only then did she dare look up at Edward. To her surprise and immense relief, he was smiling broadly.

"My, my, Lady Temper is in fine form tonight," he remarked. "Good night, Jane." As if he, too, had been reminded of his new position, he added formally, "We look forward to your company tomorrow."

* * *

Katherine was beside herself. She and Jane were to sit with their mother in Queen Katherine's box to watch the jousting! But when they finally rode onto the tournament grounds, she suffered an attack of shyness, and Jane practically had to drag her forward towards the queen's box. Jane was so busy reassuring her sister that she herself was unprepared when the queen turned and beckoned her to come forward. Hastily gathering her full, lynx-lined skirts around her, Jane hurried to obey. She dropped to a full curtsy in front of the queen, glad that today, at least, she had managed it with grace.

Queen Katherine reached out and gently raised her to her feet.

"Stand up, my little mousekin. Let me have a good look at you. Why, you are a *tiny* mousekin, aren't you?"

"Yes, your grace," Jane answered. "But I hope to grow."

The queen laughed. "I'm sure you will. And what think you about coming to live with me, my pet?" Her voice was friendly and reassuring.

"I think it a great honour your majesty's grace has bestowed upon me," Jane answered quickly. "I am very grateful to your grace." She smiled, and her whole face lit up. The queen

37

smiled back. In that instant a bond was formed that was never to be broken as long as they both lived.

"You shall be my daughter," Queen Katherine exclaimed. "And I shall consider myself fortunate to be mother to such a lovely child. The Princess Elizabeth and I look forward to having you with us."

"Thank you, your grace," Jane answered. Her heart sank a little at the mention of the Princess Elizabeth. Jane was not at all certain that she was looking forward to her arrival quite as much as was the queen.

Never mind, Jane thought to herself. Last night's incident will be forgotten. I shall make myself as amiable as possible from now on and I'm sure we shall get on. But I will never again forget to show the proper respect, she added silently. The princess obviously was one who demanded it, and she would oblige.

Just then trumpets sounded and King Edward rode onto the field, surrounded by his noblemen. He took his seat just above the queen's box and gave the signal for the activities to begin.

Jane looked around for Princess Elizabeth and Princess Mary, but the two princesses, for reasons of their own, had decided not to attend the tournament. Jane knew that their status was still uncertain. Although King Henry had, in his will, declared them as heirs after Edward, they were still officially illegitimate. During the old king's lifetime he had alternately pampered them and ignored them. The only real family life they had known had been during the marriage of the king to Katherine Parr. She had insisted they be brought back to court and had given them a loving home. The Princess Elizabeth was to remain with her now, but Mary preferred to return to her estate at Hunsdon as soon as the coronation festivities were over. It was obvious that the Catholic Mary felt uncomfortable in the increasingly Protestant atmosphere of the court.

The rest of the afternoon was a feast of colour and spectacle as the peers of the realm competed in the various jousting and tilting tournaments. Pennants flew gaily from flagstaffs, whipping and snapping in the wind. Edward leaned down continuously from his position above them to keep them well informed as to the identity of all the contestants.

"Here comes my uncle, Thomas Seymour!" he cried suddenly. "I'll wager he will despatch his opponents quite thriftily. There's not many can match him!"

The younger brother of the Protector rode on to the field. He was in full armour and sat his horse with confidence. True to Edward's predictions, he unhorsed his first opponent easily. The second gave him more trouble. On the first pass the lances thudded heavily against the shields, but while the opposing knight swayed alarmingly in the saddle, he did not fall. Turning at opposite ends of the field, the combatants made ready again. At the signal, they spurred their horses forward and charged each other — long, wooden lances held rigidly horizontal, horses' hooves tearing up great flying clods of earth.

"Will he win this time, your grace?" Katherine was so carried away she forgot her shyness and addressed Queen Katherine directly.

There was no answer. Jane took her eyes off the two madly galloping figures and glanced up. Then she stared. The queen was deathly pale and biting her lip. Her fingers tore at a handkerchief, and even as Jane watched, it shredded and came apart. The queen's eyes were riveted on Thomas Seymour. When the clash came and he remained on his horse, victorious, she relaxed and smiled brilliantly. Her cheeks flushed, then flushed even more scarlet as the Protector's brother turned, removed his helmet, and made obeisance to King Edward. He was a handsome man, with a full beard and flashing blue eyes. Jane could have sworn that, although he was facing the king, those eyes were on Queen Katherine. She was puzzled and slightly troubled for a moment, then forgot the incident as another bout was announced.

This time it was the Duke of Somerset who was to compete — the Lord Protector himself. As he made ready under his colours, Jane recognized with a start the figure who was helping him. It was the same young boy she had noticed in Edward's procession. She had seen him sitting close to Edward at the banquet the night before, but had been hesitant about asking anyone who he was. Now she seized her chance. Queen Katherine was chatting with Lady Frances, and Jane waited for a pause in the conversation. Her mother made that a bit difficult. Finally, however, she stopped to draw breath and Jane broke in hesitantly.

"If it please your grace," she began.

Her mother glared at her, but Queen Katherine turned to her immediately, looking relieved, Jane thought. She could understand that. Sometimes the Lady Frances was rather overpowering.

"What is it, mousekin?" the queen asked, smiling gently.

Jane plunged in. "The boy who is assisting the Duke of Somerset, your grace. Who is he? I saw him yesterday in the procession as well."

"Aha! So you have found someone who takes your fancy already, have you?" the queen teased.

Jane blushed. "No, no!" she protested. "I just wondered . . ."

"That's Lord Edward, Earl of Hertford," Queen Katherine answered, still laughing. "The eldest son of the Protector. He's a great friend of the king's grace — you will see quite a lot of him, I'm sure. In fact," she went on, "we'll make certain that you do. That would be a good match for you, my little mousekin, and we *will* have to start looking around, won't we?"

Jane felt as if her cheeks were on fire. "Oh, your grace! I never meant —"

Queen Katherine patted Jane on the shoulder, then turned back to Lady Frances, who was looking like a thundercloud. As soon as the queen addressed her, however, her face cleared, and with an obvious effort, she produced a falsely sweet smile.

It was very late that night when Jane finally bade her parents good night. As she left them to go up to her bed, she was stopped by her mother's shrill voice. It sounded as if her feelings had been pent up all day and now, at last, they had burst forth — after Jane was out of sight, but before she was out of earshot.

"Marriage to the Earl of Hertford indeed!" the Lady Frances almost shouted.

Jane paused, knowing she should go on, but impelled by a curiosity beyond her control to hear what her mother was saying.

"With all respect to the queen, I have in mind a far higher marriage than that!"

"Perhaps, my lady, you aim too high." Jane's father's voice was placating, nervous.

"Too high! How should I aim too high? Jane is of royal blood. Why should she not make a royal marriage? It would be entirely fitting. Entirely logical, under the circumstances."

Jane froze. Her mother could not possibly mean— her blood chilled. Suddenly a terrible sense of foreboding overcame her, and she fled to the safety of her room as if the devil were at her heels.

4
Uneasy beginnings

It snowed the day Katherine, Lord Dorset, and
Lady Frances left to return to Bradgate. Jane
bade them farewell from the steps of Chelsea Palace, then stood watching after them until they
were long out of sight. A totally unfamiliar
feeling of loneliness overwhelmed her.

"My lady! You'll catch your death out here!"

Jane turned towards her familiar, chiding
old nurse with relief and meekly allowed herself
to be led indoors.

After all the excitement of the coronation,
life at Chelsea Palace was quiet. This suited Jane
completely. She soon settled into a routine. A
tutor had been hired for her — John Aylmer —
and she liked the young man immediately. He
was a close friend to Roger Ascham, the brilliant
tutor of Princess Elizabeth. Learning was taken
very seriously for high-born ladies at this time;
they were expected to apply themselves to it
during most of their waking hours. By nine years
old Jane had already learned Greek and Latin,
and had a good working knowledge of Spanish,
Italian, and French. She also loved music with a
passion and played the lute, harp, and cithern.

When the queen informed her that part of her court education would be to learn the court galliards and pavanes, and the symbolism underlying all the intricate movements of these dances, she was delighted.

One thing only bothered Jane — the attitude of Princess Elizabeth. The princess did not criticize her again, but neither did she respond to Jane's tentative offers of friendship.

"She treats me as if she wished I weren't here," Jane complained one day as Mrs. Ellen helped her dress. "Why does she dislike me so?"

"I don't think she dislikes you at all, my lady," the old nurse responded. "You must remember, my lady, the princess has had a difficult life. I would not take it upon myself to criticize the king's grace, but —"

She paused, and Jane waited. Mrs. Ellen was fond of stating that she "would not take it upon herself to criticize" somebody, then usually ended up doing so anyway. Just as Jane had known she would, Mrs. Ellen continued, but in a cautious whisper.

"Our dear King Henry, God rest his soul, was perhaps a trifle hard on her. At first he loved her with a passion and was *so* proud of her. He made much of her and insisted that she be brought to dandle on his knee at all the court functions. Never was there a child so petted and coddled. Then, when her unfortunate mother was executed and the king married again and was blessed with a son, he turned against the poor little princess entirely. He sent her away, as he had sent Princess Mary away before her, and, I've

44

been told, hardly provided enough to keep the child clothed and fed. It's only natural, I suppose, that the princess should be a little reserved — nervous, I should think, about what may befall her next."

"But *I'm* no threat to her," Jane protested. Nevertheless, with this she had to be satisfied.

* * *

It was almost a month before a summons came for Jane to attend upon the king again, this time at Whitehall Palace where he was staying. They would go by barge, of course, as both Chelsea Palace and Whitehall were on the banks of the Thames River. It was much easier to travel by water than to brave the muddy paths and hordes of people that would obstruct their way by land. Luckily, the day was mild. There was even a hint of spring in the air, although the wind off the river was chill. Small irises and the first tips of crocuses were just beginning to appear in the gardens.

Jane lifted her long skirts carefully up out of the wet, and accepted the helping hands of two young pages as she stepped down the slippery, moss-covered water stairs into the barge. Around her the river was full of traffic — sailing barges, rowing barges, and the little rowing boats called wherries. She leaned forward eagerly as they moved away from shore, anxious to see all there was to be seen — she had never travelled by river before. Queen Katherine sat beside her and took great delight in pointing out everything of interest as they sailed swiftly down the river. The

Princess Elizabeth sat by Jane's other side, looking more relaxed and happy than she usually did.

Suddenly there was a commotion ahead of them. The boatmen let out cries of warning and began to pull in the sails quickly as they saw that the river was jammed with boats. Men were standing up, tipping their crafts perilously, yelling and shouting at something in the middle of it all.

"What is it, boatman?" Queen Katherine asked.

"It's a bear, your grace!" he answered, a wide grin on his face. "They're having a bear-baiting on the water! Does your grace wish us to go closer?"

"Most certainly," the queen replied. "Now, Jane, you will see some sport. Watch carefully. If he is a good bear, he will give those fine lads some difficulties. Bear-baiting in a boat is no easy matter."

As they drew nearer and the other boatmen became aware of them, a path was cleared for their barge. "The queen!" the shout went up. "Make way for her grace, Queen Katherine!" The cheers mingled with the frenzied shouts of those who were tormenting the bear.

The animal was standing on its two hind paws, a heavy chain dangling from a collar around its neck. Its keeper was hanging onto the end of the chain, looking none too happy about what was going on. The unfortunate bear was surrounded by men in other barges who where prodding and poking at it with oars, sticks, and makeshift spears. The bear was hitting out at the weapons, bellowing with rage. A stream of blood poured from a wound in one shoulder.

"The poor animal," Jane murmured, horrified at the cruelty.

"It is just a beast," Princess Elizabeth declared, shrugging. "A bear is no more than a beast."

"Surely even beasts can feel pain. And terror," Jane answered, more sharply than she had intended.

"They'll be taking it over to the bear-baiting arena in Southwark," one of the pages spoke to her breathlessly. "Some of the men in the other barges are just determined to have a little sport with it on the way, my lady. Oh, look!" he cried suddenly. "Oh, my lady! It's loose!"

The bear had torn its chain out of the keeper's hands and seemed intent on charging its tormentors.

"Away! Away with the bear!" came the terrified shout as the animal lunged into a small wherry beside the barge that was carrying it. The wherry was immediately swamped. Its owner leaped into the dark brown, fetid current as his boat sank beneath him. In a moment the bear was in the water beside him.

As they swept past the scene of wild confusion, Jane saw the man hauled unceremoniously out of the river. The bear was swimming madly around in circles, attacking first one boat, then another.

"Oh, wait!" she cried out to the boatman.

"Stop! I want to see what happens!" But even as she spoke, the boat sped by.

"They'll swim him to the side if the others get out of the way," the page assured her with a confident air. "Bears swim very well, my lady."

Jane looked down at him with gratitude. He, at least, was trying to comfort her. Out of all the others in the boat — even the kind-hearted Queen Katherine herself — he seemed to be the only one who understood how she felt. His words helped to ease her distress a little.

When they arrived at Whitehall Palace, Queen Katherine disappeared to her own apartments, which she still retained next to the king's. The Princess Elizabeth went with her.

"Stay you here and await his majesty's summons, Jane," the queen said. "I know he is anxious to see you."

Within moments a footman appeared and bowed. "Will you follow me, my lady?"

Jane followed him to the king's presence chamber, her lips set. She was determined not to make any errors today. As soon as she was ushered into the room, she sank into a well-rehearsed curtsy and stayed there, eyes held rigidly on the carpet at her feet.

"Jane!" It was a glad cry. "You are well come, my dear cousin. Come and meet these good people."

Jane looked up to find the warm, tapestry-hung room seemingly full of people. It took her a moment to sort them out, then she realized that there were not so many after all. Footmen and pages stood in attendance around the room, and three boys lounged on stools at Edward's feet.

One of them was the other Edward, son of the Protector. He was tossing a ball idly for the king's little dog. As Jane looked at him, he returned her glance mischievously, then rolled the ball towards her. The dog ran after it, but just as he was about to pounce on it, he changed his mind and attacked Jane's skirt furiously instead. She stared down at the growling mass of fur and wondered what she should do. Somehow or other she didn't think it would be proper to seize the king's puppy by the scruff of the neck and shake it as she would have done one of her own dogs if it had been so naughty. But it was her best gown. She winced as she heard the fabric tear. Mrs. Ellen would have a fit!

"Here, Tomkins! Here!" Edward called to the dog laughingly, but it paid him no attention at all. A kingly command obviously didn't impress this small subject.

"Pull him off, Edward, do. You're the one who set him on our cousin."

The Protector's son rose and obligingly removed the pup, grinning amiably at Jane as he did so. She smiled back in spite of herself.

"My lady," the king announced, "you must meet my three best friends. Edward, my cousin" — Edward bowed formally — "and my dear friends, Henry Sidney and Barnaby Fitzpatrick." The young king was still laughing and obviously disposed to do away with any undo formality this time.

The afternoon passed swiftly with music and

lively conversation. Queen Katherine joined them after a while, then Princess Elizabeth came as well. She seemed pleased to see her brother again and, although formal as always, today she laughed and talked as much as the others.

"Have some more honeycakes, Lady Jane." Barnaby Fitzpatrick suddenly appeared at Jane's elbow, platter in hand. "I hear you are very clever, my lady," he whispered impishly in her ear as he held it out. "Even more clever than the Princess Elizabeth, that paragon of virtue and learning!"

Jane looked at him, shocked, almost upsetting the dish of cakes as she did so. She saw that he was grinning broadly and immediately suspected she was being teased.

"Of course not! You mustn't say such things!" She cast an anxious glance in the princess's direction. The last thing she needed was for the princess to hear talk of that sort!

"More clever," he repeated, "and prettier too. The king's grace says so himself."

Jane blushed and tried in vain to hush him. There was a devilish glint in his black eyes, however, and the grin on his small, pointed face was even more wicked.

"You are mocking me!" Jane shot back in a furious whisper. "Pray stop immediately or we shall both suffer for it."

"Nay, Lady Jane. I would not dream of mocking you. I think you are one of the fairest maidens I have ever seen. And I'm not alone in my thoughts either. Have you not noticed how our dear king's cousin, Lord Edward, glances at you? The king's grace assures me he is quite smitten. Ever since he saw you at the coronation."

Jane was totally at a loss for words. Involuntarily she looked over towards where the Protector's son was sitting. He was looking at the two of them curiously. To Jane's horror, she felt her cheeks redden even more as he rose and started to come over. A stir at the door made him pause, as a footman ushered in two more visitors. Jane turned away from the roguish Barnaby thankfully, and dropped to a curtsy as she recognized the Lord Protector himself, closely followed by his younger brother.

As Jane rose again, her eyes fell upon the queen. A flush had come to her cheeks as well. Her eyes were bright and fixed on Thomas Seymour so intently she seemed to have forgotten there was anyone else in the room at all. The king's younger uncle, however, took no notice of her and wore an expression which looked almost sulking as he followed his brother into the room.

"Your grace," the Duke of Somerset said, as he bowed to Queen Katherine, "you will forgive this interruption, I pray, but there are matters which can wait no longer for the king's attention."

"Oh, Uncle," Edward objected, "surely there is nothing that we cannot attend to later?"

"The emissary from France is here, your grace. We cannot keep him waiting any longer."

Queen Katherine, who had torn her eyes away from Thomas Seymour with a start when the duke had addressed her, rose to her feet.

"With your grace's kind consent, we will be retiring," she said to Edward. "With your permission, we will attend upon you tomorrow."

Jane rose as well, but her own eyes strayed back to the Protector's son. Barnaby's words were still echoing in her mind. Smitten? Had he really said smitten? Edward was standing rigidly behind his father and uncle now, his face serious, his demeanour obedient. He looked at Jane out of the corner of his eye. She jumped. Was it possible he had winked at her?

*   *   *

The next morning something happened that confused and upset Jane. A lady-in-waiting came to tell her that the queen would like Jane to attend her, but when Jane made to enter the queen's presence room she stopped short. A man was already there, pacing from one end of the room to the other with long, furious strides.

"I most humbly apologize, your grace," he was saying. "My behaviour yesterday was abominable." It was the Protector's younger brother, Thomas Seymour. In spite of his words, however, he seemed more angry than apologetic.

"Lord High Admiral of the Navy, the Lord Protector has made me!" he exploded. "My dear brother awards me with sops, while he keeps all the power to himself!"

"So it is power you want so badly, my dear friend," the queen answered gently. "I had heard . . . rumours . . . that you were perhaps seeking to marry in very high places."

The Protector's brother stopped in mid-stride and looked at her. "Your grace —" he began.

"The names of both princesses were mentioned," the queen went on. Her voice was still gentle, but there was a strained sound to it. She was hugging her arms tightly across her breast — as if she were holding herself together, keeping herself from flying apart.

"Your grace!" He was down on his knees before her in a flash. "Who could have brought you these lies? How could your grace believe —" He grasped her hand and covered it with kisses, feverishly. "Your grace knows there has never been anyone else. Never *could* be anyone else!"

Queen Katherine withdrew her hand and turned away. Her body had relaxed, however, and she let out a deep sigh.

"I believe you. Of course I believe you. But you must not speak so. It is too soon . . ."

Jane took a few steps backwards with only one thought in mind — escape! Before the queen saw her!

There was no escaping the presence of the Lord High Admiral of England at Chelsea Palace during the next few weeks, however. He was a constant visitor. And always, when he was there, the queen brightened. It seemed to Jane that she had turned back time itself and was becoming more youthful every day. At first Jane rejoiced with her. Some of her misgivings about the scene she had witnessed between the two had been assuaged by her nurse, Mrs. Ellen. Through her, Jane learned that the queen had been promised to Thomas Seymour before King Henry had taken a fancy to her. Once the king had chosen her, however, there was nothing they could do. The king's will ruled above all else.

"It does seem romantic," Mrs. Ellen had sighed, and Jane had agreed with her. The Lord High Admiral was a handsome man, with a charm and gaiety that could not be denied. He filled corners with his laughter and warmed spirits with his good humour. Not once did he let slip any hint of dissatisfaction. But every now and then, when Jane caught him off guard, she was sure she could see the sulky, calculating look he had worn that afternoon at Whitehall Palace. Gradually, not even knowing why, Jane began to trust him less and less.

But in this growing dislike she was alone. Rumour had it that young King Edward doted on him. The Lord High Admiral danced attendance upon Edward whenever he was not dancing attendance upon Queen Katherine, and lavished presents upon him extravagantly. Even the usually solemn Princess Elizabeth responded to him. She laughed and joked with him more openly than with any other person. The queen seemed delighted by this warm side to Elizabeth's character and encouraged her.

Jane chided herself reproachfully for seeing anything wrong with this. For imagining sometimes that the princess was more than just friendly with the queen's suitor. For seeing something between the two that could not possibly be there. It must only be her imagination.

But it was with a happiness more feigned than real that Jane congratulated her beloved queen when Katherine came to her one morning with a radiant face.

"We have sought permission from the king's grace, my little mousekin, and he has granted it. The Lord High Admiral and I are to be married!"

5
Clouds gather

The wedding took place in May. It was a very
quiet affair, almost secret. Many people did not
know about it until it was over. The queen worried because it was so soon after King Henry's
death, but the Lord High Admiral was insistent,
and she was obviously too much in love with him
to hold out against his wishes for long. The
summer that followed was so happy for her that
Jane was encouraged to put aside her misgivings.

The boisterous, booming presence of the Lord
High Admiral effected a great change in their
lives. Studies went on as usual, but mealtimes
were noisier and happier, and the queen began to
entertain more and more often. The most striking
change was in the Princess Elizabeth. For perhaps the first time since her childhood, she
seemed to relax and allow herself to feel secure in
the warm, happy, family setting. Thomas Seymour made no secret of his affection and admiration for her, and she made no secret of her
fondness for him. This comfortable state of affairs
delighted the queen. Indeed, she joined in with
the admiral in merry romps with the young princess that would leave the three of them breath-

less with laughter. At times the extent of these romps shocked the prim Mrs. Ellen.

"It's not proper, my lady," she muttered one day as Jane was making ready for bed. "Although it's not my place to say it, it's not proper."

Jane, who had spent the day wrestling with a particularly difficult Greek translation, looked at her old nurse with mild exasperation. "What's not proper? What *are* you fussing about now, madam?" She didn't really want to know, didn't really want to hear anything that might make her worry about the status of their outwardly tranquil family life.

Jane was happier now than she could ever remember being. She missed her sisters and Bradgate Park, but could not bring herself to miss her strict, demanding parents overly much. The studious, calm life she had found with Queen Katherine suited her far more. The queen had introduced her to Dr. Latimer — one of the most intellectual advocates of Protestantism Jane had ever met — and she had taken a great delight in talking with him. King Edward also shared her passion for the new religion, and the three of them, with Sir John Cheke, Edward's tutor — who was also an ardent Protestant — had spent hours discussing and studying it.

There was no stopping Mrs. Ellen, however.

"Although it's not my place to say it," she repeated, "it's scandalous to allow a gentleman the freedom of a young lady's bedchamber like that."

Jane kept silent, hoping the impossible

would happen and Mrs. Ellen would not go on. It didn't.

"Every morning the Lord High Admiral and the queen herself go in to wake up her highness, the princess, and Mrs. Ashley says they make great sport with her — tickling and tumbling her around in her bed until she is quite breathless with laughter! And this morning the admiral went in to wake her by himself. Mrs. Ashley even saw him give the princess a slap on the buttocks as she ran from him, and he jested with her most coarsely!"

Jane looked at her. She wished she could believe Mrs. Ellen was exaggerating, but she knew only too well that what she spoke was the truth. How could the queen countenance such goings on? And the princess — the usually so formal and so restrained Princess Elizabeth — what had gotten into her? With an annoyed frown, Jane turned away from her nurse.

"Hold your tongue, Mrs. Ellen, do. It ill becomes you to gossip so."

Unfortunately, the first person Jane ran into the next morning was the admiral himself. "God's bones, my little lady, but you are looking particularly lovely this morn!" he bellowed amiably.

Jane fixed him with a sour look and lowered her brows. "Your language does not become you, my lord," she said.

"My apologies, milady," the admiral laughed. "I see your mood does not match your appearance."

Jane was not to be teased back into good humour, however. She brushed by him quickly.

58

*   *   *

A frequent visitor at Chelsea Palace that summer was the Lord Protector's son, Edward. Queen Katherine invited him whenever possible, and he never refused an invitation. Jane looked forward to his visits more and more as the summer wore on. She visited often with her cousin, King Edward, also, and soon was thinking of him almost as more of a brother than a cousin. The summer passed quickly — truly one of the happiest Jane could ever remember.

By the autumn a few clouds had begun to gather. Following the dictates of Protestantism, King Edward's Privy Council had passed many laws changing the old Catholic services in the churches. Statues and images had been removed, altars torn down, stained glass windows broken or replaced. The once colourful interiors were now plain and whitewashed, in keeping with the Protestant desire for simplicity, for direct contact with God instead of intercession through the Saints and the Virgin Mary. For many of the people these changes were unwelcome and frightening, and they could not accept them. The Protestants, for their part, insisted on them. Finally violence erupted one cold, blustery November day.

"Cousin, have you heard what is happening?" Jane was alone with King Edward and availed herself of the informality he allowed when there was no one else present.

"I have," the king replied. He and Jane had celebrated their tenth birthday together the month before. He was a child still, in years, but the frown on his face was not childish. "My uncle and Archbishop Cranmer say not to worry. That it will all be for the best."

"Surely it is not all for the best when apprentices and the lower sorts of people revile priests, even though they do be Catholics?"

"The priests must learn the new ways, Jane. They must change."

"Yes, of course," Jane agreed. "But still, they are men of God, even though misguided, and they are being attacked — even tossed in blankets and beaten. Surely that cannot be right!"

Edward had not answered her, and in the following days, with all the preparations for the Christmas celebrations, the matter was not mentioned again.

This Christmas was to be a Tudor family reunion. The Princess Mary was coming from Hunsdon to join her brother and sister. There were to be balls, masques, feasts, and merry-making of all kinds. Jane was included in everything, and for the time being, studies were put aside. Her favourite partner for all the dances was, of course, the young Lord Edward, son of the Protector. She enjoyed his company so much she didn't even mind the inevitable teasing.

"I shall have to be speaking to your parents soon about this match," Queen Katherine laughed as they returned to Chelsea Palace late one day.

Jane laughed with her. Marriage itself did not particularly interest her yet, but she knew that it was necessary, and the time for the settling of her person could not be far off. If it had to be, she thought contentedly — and it certainly did have to be — it might just as well be Edward. It could be a lot worse. One of her cousins had been married at thirteen years of age to an old man of sixty who had the gout, and she had spent her first year of married life running and fetching for him and nursing him. Mercifully, he had died at the beginning of the second year.

Suddenly Jane remembered what she had overheard her mother say about her marriage. For a moment the sense of foreboding she had felt then overcame her again. She shivered, then pushed it out of her mind. Her mother could not have meant what Jane had thought she meant. She must have misheard her. Marriage to the Protector's son would be an excellent match. Even her conniving parents would have to admit that!

The question of the religion of England could not be put aside for long. It was decided that Lent would be observed as usual, and to forestall further unrest, Parliament attended both Catholic and Protestant Communion services. By spring another unrest had surfaced to add to the turmoil. Many people were objecting to the enclosing of common lands by the great lords for their own purposes. In this matter the Duke of Somerset sided with the people against his own peers. Much to their annoyance, but with King Edward's full acceptance, he tried to set an example to them by having the great lands of Hampton Court disparked. The Tudors had hunted and sported in these great parks for years; the opening of them to the public was an unprecedented move. The common people cheered the "good duke," but the lords of the Privy Council grumbled behind their beards.

"Your father is a great man, Edward," Jane remarked. "He truly feels for the people."

"I wish sometimes he would feel more for himself," Edward answered. "He has made many enemies by this move, Jane."

No one could remain concerned for long, however, in the bright, warm, spring atmosphere of the court. When the queen announced that she was pregnant, there was no thought in anyone's mind but of rejoicing and celebration.

*   *   *

"Jane, my sweet, have you seen the Princess Elizabeth?" Queen Katherine looked up from her embroidery one morning as Jane came to sit with her for a while before dinner. "Mr. Ascham is waiting for her. It's not like her to be late for lessons."

"She is in her room, I believe, your grace," Jane answered. "Shall I send a page for her?"

"No, mousekin, thank you. I am going up to my own chamber to lie down for a while. I'll call her myself." The queen was in her fifth month of pregnancy and tired easily. The doctors were worried about her, Jane knew, as they felt that her grace was too old to be bearing her first child. Still, her happiness was such that worry had to be cast aside.

Jane settled down to a piece of embroidery of her own. To her annoyance, she found she had left some of the threads up in her room. No one but Mrs. Ellen would know where they were and she wasn't around, so with a sigh of exasperation, Jane rose to go and fetch them herself. As she reached the long hall upstairs, she suddenly heard the queen's voice. It was not her usual soft, gentle tone, however. Her words were actually shrill and loud enough to carry clearly back to where Jane was standing.

"My lady! My lord husband! What is the meaning of this?"

The queen was standing outside the door to the princess's bedchamber. To Jane's consternation, the Lord High Admiral himself suddenly emerged from the room and appeared beside the queen in the doorway. He was flushed and dishevelled.

"My love!" he exclaimed. "Calm yourself, my love. Remember the babe you carry. You must not excite yourself so!"

"If you do not wish me to excite myself, sirrah, then perhaps you will explain the scene I just witnessed." The queen had controlled herself with an obvious effort, and now her voice was icily cool.

"A friendly embrace, my love. Such as a father gives to his child. 'Twas no more. Surely, my love, you have seen me do as much when you yourself have been present."

"Not *quite* as much. And I was *not* present." Without a further word, the queen turned on her heel and went on to her own room. The admiral made haste to hurry after her.

Jane decided to practise her music instead of

doing embroidery, and raced back down the stairs. From the princess, in her room, there came not a sound.

The Princess Elizabeth did not appear for supper that evening. The queen herself went up to her room and stayed there with her for a long time. The next day, when they were assembling for dinner, Queen Katherine appeared with the princess, one arm affectionately encircling her shoulders. Princess Elizabeth appeared much more subdued than she had been of late, but the queen was back to her usual loving, kind self.

"Jane, my mousekin," she announced gaily, "we are to make some changes. My lord husband feels that the air in Gloucestershire will be healthier for me during my last months, so next month we shall be removing to his estate there, Sudeley Castle. The princess wishes to visit her dear friends Sir Anthony and Lady Denny at Cheshunt, but I do hope you will accompany us and be my companion while we await our new babe's birth?"

"Of course, your grace," Jane answered. "It will be my pleasure." But there was hesitation in her voice.

"Are you thinking you will miss the company of your gallant suitor?" the queen teased lightly, looking at Jane's somewhat dubious face.

Jane blushed. That was exactly what she had been thinking.

"He will write to you, I'm certain of it. And after the babe is born and is old enough to travel, we'll come back. We'll be back for Christmas, and won't we just have a celebration then?" She hugged Elizabeth to include her in the happy invitation.

Jane was relieved. The queen's icy behaviour the day before had been so unlike her — it had been frightening.

Within a month the preparations for the removal were complete, and Jane began yet another journey. They travelled more slowly than Jane had on her way to London, with the queen resting as comfortably as possible in a horse-drawn litter.

It was a bright, hot day in full midsummer when they arrived at Sudeley Castle. Servants and townsfolk from the whole district had assembled to greet them. Banners flew, and there was such an air of holiday excitement about the event that it seemed more like a jousting tournament. For a moment Jane felt a pang of regret. Her Edward would probably be attending a real jousting tournament, possibly at this very moment. This year he would go in the lists himself. He had been so excited and proud. And Jane had wanted so much to be there to see him.

Never mind, she told herself. It won't be long until we return. And for now my duty lies with the queen.

The rest of the summer passed in a lazy haze. However, the queen tired more and more easily and dark circles seemed permanently etched under her eyes. Jane knew the doctors were afraid things were not going well. She worried, but there was nothing more she could do other than attend to the queen and help make her as comfortable as possible.

One morning in late August, the Lord High Admiral appeared in the queen's chambers dressed for riding.

"Are you travelling yet again, my lord?" the queen asked. There was a plaintive note in her voice that was new.

Jane looked up from where she was sitting in the corner. Her heart ached with sympathy for her queen. The Lord High Admiral seemed to spend most of his time away these days.

"My love," he answered. His voice was tender, but there was an air of haste about him that belied his words. "Your grace knows I would not leave you at this time if it were not a matter of the utmost urgency, but I am the Lord High Admiral, your grace knows, and I do have duties to attend to."

The queen sighed. "It's only . . . I feel my time is very near. I would you were here."

"And I will be, I promise you. I will be." He bent to kiss the queen's hand, then turned on his heel and rushed out.

Jane looked after him, hardly able to conceal the dislike she felt for him.

Less than a week later, in the middle of the night, a maidservant ran to Jane's room, screaming hysterically. "It's the babe, my lady," she cried. "It's coming!"

"Hush your noise," Jane scolded her with all the authority she could muster. With a cold, sinking feeling, she realized that with the admiral away she was in charge. Old Lady Seymour, the admiral's mother, was the only other member of the family there, and she was too doddering and silly to be of any use whatsoever.

"Has the doctor been sent for?"

"Yes, my lady."

"And the Lord High Admiral?"

"Yes, my lady."

"Then have Mrs. Ellen called and come quickly to her grace's room. And stop snivelling! Babes are born every day. Her grace will have no trouble at all, I'm sure."

But Jane was far from sure. In fact, she was terrified. She had never assisted at a birthing and had no idea what to expect. It was with tremendous relief that she welcomed the doctor when he arrived.

By the next day, however, the relief had evaporated. The birth was not going well. The queen was in constant pain, and the doctor seemed to know no more about what to do than did Jane. To make matters worse, the admiral had not yet appeared. If it had not been for the steady reassurance of Mrs. Ellen, the whole household would have fallen apart.

Finally the Lord High Admiral did arrive. He seemed more annoyed at having been called back than worried about the queen, however.

"Her grace, the queen, is not well —" Jane began when he dismounted. She had been waiting impatiently for him in the hall.

"I'll go to her as soon as I have changed," the admiral answered shortly.

"My lord, she is not well at all. I fear she is dying!" All the composure Jane had been trying to maintain broke and to her horror she began to cry.

"Nonsense!" he exclaimed. "The doctor is with her, is he not? Enough of these women's hysterics. I will attend upon her grace as soon as I am ready."

But by the time the admiral was ready, it was over. The baby was born, and it was a girl.

"A girl?" The incredulity and disappointment were only too evident.

"Hush, my lord. She will hear you. Thank God she has survived and is all right!" Jane greeted the admiral in the antechamber to the queen's room. "Will you go in now, my lord? Then we can pray together and give thanks that her grace has survived. I was so worried, my lord. She was in such pain."

"But . . . a girl! All this fuss and pother for a girl!" The admiral made no attempt at all to lower his voice.

Jane winced and glared at him. The dislike she had felt before amounted almost to hatred now. At least the queen is all right, she thought silently. Thanks be to our most merciful God that she is all right.

But Jane's thanks were premature. Six days after the frail, weak, baby girl was born, Queen Kathcrine Parr died.

*   *   *

"Surely, my lord, you are not leaving before the funeral?" Jane stared at the Lord High Admiral, aghast. It was only the day after the queen had died.

"I must. Urgent business calls me to London. I must see the king immediately."

"Urgent business, indeed!" Jane stormed as soon as she was in the privacy of her own room. "Urgent business to see what can be done to keep his nest well feathered now that he is no longer husband to the queen!" The strain and tragedy of the past week finally caught up to her and she threw herself on her bed. Sobs welled up — she could make no further effort to stifle them. She wept until the physical pain of weeping was almost more than she could bear.

"Hush, my lady. Hush." Mrs. Ellen sat down beside Jane, then held her and rocked her as she had not done for a long time. But Jane could not hush. Nor could she stop weeping. The person she had loved most dearly in all the world was gone. And the person *she* had loved most dearly had not even bothered to stay for her funeral.

And so it was that the diminutive figure of Lady Jane Grey led the long procession into the chapel as chief mourner at her beloved queen's funeral. The funeral was elaborate, befitting the widow of a great king. The chapel was transformed with heraldic banners and black-draped cloths. Hundreds of people — nobles and commoners alike — had come to Sudeley Castle to do reverence to their beloved queen. Above Jane, held by six ushers in black surcoats, swayed the canopy of state, embroidered with the arms of the Tudors and the Seymours. Jane walked in royal splendour, but she walked alone, muffled in the trappings of woe and clothed in the black of death.

6

"You will pay for this, Uncle!"

After the funeral Jane was sent to join her parents who were now back at Dorset House in London. They were none too pleased to see her. It was clear their plans had been disrupted, and they did not seem certain of what to do next. Jane herself felt lost and bereft. To add to her loneliness, her sister Katherine had not been allowed to come to London this time.

Then one day a little less than a month later, she heard a familiar booming voice as she came down the stairs to join her parents for dinner.

"Marry, it is settled then," the jovial tones of the Lord High Admiral announced. "You shall have five hundred pounds immediately as first payment of two thousand pounds for the wardship of my Lady Jane. I promise you'll have no cause to regret this, Dorset. The betrothal is as good as accomplished."

As Jane stood, thunderstruck, on the bottom stair, her mother swept into view, closely followed by Lord Dorset and the admiral.

"My lady!" the admiral exclaimed, hastening

to bow and kiss her hand with elaborate courtesy. "It seems I am to have the delightful pleasure of your company once again. My home at Seymour Place awaits your coming. I will have a suite of rooms decorated for you that will be suitable for a princess — nay, suitable for a queen!"

Before the astonished Jane could answer, he straightened and, with a flourish of his heavy riding cloak, was gone.

Jane turned to her parents. "What is the meaning of this, good my lord father and lady mother?"

"You are to return to live with his lordship, the admiral," her mother replied archly. "He has graciously agreed to accept you as his ward."

"For payment of five hundred pounds, first payment of two thousand pounds!"

Lady Frances coloured and her plump cheeks trembled with rage. "How dare you speak to your parents in that fashion, mistress? Your lord father and I are the ones to determine what is best for you. You will obey us without question!"

"And the betrothal my lord spoke of, what betrothal did he mean? What have you been conspiring with him?"

"Be quiet!" Jane's father grabbed her by the arm and shook her harshly. "Hold your tongue! There was no talk of betrothal. You are to become the Lord High Admiral's ward, that is all. Hold your tongue!"

Behind his fury, Jane saw a glint of fear in his eyes. They were conspiring something secret. And something dangerous also, if it could not be

71

spoken of openly. It could only be one thing. They *were* planning to marry her to the king. And if the Lord High Admiral was arranging it, it could only be in order to further his own interests. Jane knew him well enough by now to know that his thoughts were solely for himself, for the furthering of his own power. If she were the admiral's ward and she were to become queen . . . If that were to happen, then the admiral would have power equal to or even surpassing his brother's, the Lord Protector. She and her family would be indebted to him. Would owe him the greatest of favours.

"I refuse." Jane pulled her arm out of her father's grasp haughtily and made as if to turn away. "I refuse to return to the care of the Lord High Admiral. Besides, without the queen there it would not be seemly."

"You *what?*" The Lady Frances's face coloured even more, to a deep and ominous purple. Her arm drew back and she slapped Jane full across the face. The sound of the slap echoed in the silence that followed.

"Go to your room!" Her father looked as if he too were about to hit her.

Jane shrank back, her momentary courage deserting her. She made one last attempt. "It would not be seemly —"

"Lady Seymour, the admiral's mother, will be there, and he has retained all Queen Katherine's maids and ladies to wait upon you. He has gone to much expense and trouble for you, you ungrateful wench." Her father grabbed her arm again and squeezed so tightly Jane knew there would be a bruise there the next day. "To your room, I say, and make ready. You will leave as soon as possible!"

* * *

The admiral was true to his word. The rooms Jane was given at Seymour Place were suited to a queen. Her bedchamber was hung with brilliantly embroidered tapestries, the floors were covered with costly Turkish carpets, and the bed itself was draped with royal blue silk curtains. Her ladies' room, adjoining it, was hardly less sumptuous.

Jane recognized most of the ladies from her stay with Queen Katherine, but one of them was new. She was a young girl, only a few years older than Jane herself. She came up to Jane hesitantly as she saw her standing by the bed with a frown on her face.

"My lady is not pleased with her chamber?" she asked.

"The chamber pleases me. I am not pleased to be *in* it," Jane answered sharply. Then she remembered herself and bit back any further words of complaint. She looked at the young girl curiously. The girl was pretty, with soft brown curls surrounding a pleasant face with a dimple in the chin. Jane felt herself warming towards her immediately. "What is your name?" she asked.

"Elizabeth Tylney," the girl answered. "At least, that's my name now. Until a few months ago it was Elizabeth Borrows, but my father married me off to a man older than himself on my

73

fourteenth birthday, my lady." She made a face, then added quickly. "Not that my husband isn't a good man. I can have no complaint about that. He is an honest squire and generous with me to a fault — but so old!" She sighed. "Still, there's naught we can do about our fate, is there, my lady?"

Jane didn't answer.

"I was so delighted when Lady Seymour sent for me to attend upon your ladyship," Elizabeth Tylney went on, smiling again. "My older sister was lady-in-waiting to the old lady for many years, and Lady Seymour remembers her fondly. She thought you might like to have someone around closer to your own age."

Jane revised her opinion of Lady Seymour immediately. She had not thought the old lady would be so kind. There was something about the girl, too, that reminded Jane of her own dear sister, Katherine. She missed her; it would be comforting to have a friend near her own age.

"You are welcome, Mistress Tylney," Jane said. "I'm grateful for your company."

Jane's studies with her tutor, Mr. Aylmer, continued uninterrupted. Perhaps the best feature of living with the admiral, as far as Jane was concerned, and one which went far towards making up for the resentment she felt at being forced to do so, was the fact that she was close to the court and was able to visit frequently with her cousin, the king. She also saw much of the Protector's son at the palace, although the Lord High Admiral was careful never to invite his nephew to his house. He tried to discourage

Jane's friendship with him as well, for reasons which Jane was certain she knew.

Nothing more had been said about any betrothal for Jane, however. Whatever machinations the admiral was carrying on were being carried on in secret. Jane pushed the whole matter out of her mind completely, hoping only that the Lord Admiral would find something else with which to concern himself.

Then one evening she received a fright. She and King Edward were playing Trump — a game of which Edward was inordinately fond. Jane had just won a second round, and the score was tied between them, when Edward spoke.

"I think we should marry, Jane — what say you? We are so alike in thoughts and sympathies."

Jane looked up at her cousin, startled. Had he heard anything of his uncle's conniving? Was he trying to warn her? For a moment her heart stopped.

"But, no, it's a well-stuffed and jewelled princess they'll choose for me," Edward went on with a sigh as he gathered up the cards. "It's not for a king to marry whomsoever he chooses, alas."

Jane's heart started beating again as he smiled wistfully at her. She smiled in return and bent back to the cards. But Edward's words had awakened the fear in her again.

The admiral himself joined them very shortly after this exchange. Jane was startled at the informality of his entrance. Although he bowed several times to the king, his attitude was much more that of an indulgent uncle than of a subject towards his king.

"We will leave for Seymour Place within the hour, an it please your ladyship," he said lightly to Jane after he had spoken with the king for a while.

Jane glanced up at him briefly, coldly. "Very well, my lord," she answered shortly.

"Jane," Edward began after the admiral had left, "it seems you do not like our uncle over-much, is't true?" He was looking at her curiously.

Jane looked back at him levelly. She never felt the need to dissimulate with Edward. "No, I do not. It is not by my choice that I stay with him."

"But why? When we are so alike in so many things, why do we differ in this? I find the admiral a lively man, much more so than my other uncle, the Lord Protector, who is always doom and gloom and worry over every little matter. And besides, the admiral is always giving me presents. And money, thank goodness! He is very generous with his loans."

"Money!" Jane exclaimed. "But you're the king! Whatever need would you have of money?"

"King I may be, cousin, and wealthier than any other man in the kingdom, but it's precious little I ever see of my wealth. My Lord Protector keeps a tight hold on the purse strings, and I would never have coins enough to pay for favours or buy treats if it weren't for my dear uncle, the admiral."

Jane looked at Edward thoughtfully. If that

were so, then Edward must be deep in the admiral's debt. What game *was* the man playing?

*   *   *

It was Christmas again, and although neither of the princesses would attend this year, the festivities planned would be even greater than those of the previous year.

"I must say I don't miss Lady Temper's presence overly much," Edward remarked to Jane. "She likes to keep to herself. But I would like to see my other sister, the Princess Mary. She sends presents and writes to me affectionately, but she will not come."

"It is because she insists on remaining Papist," Jane remarked, unable to keep the note of disapproval out of her voice, even though she was speaking of the king's elder sister. "She cannot celebrate Mass here in her own way." The Princess Mary's insistence on remaining Catholic was beginning to prove troublesome to King Edward as the religious reformations continued, Jane knew.

"True," he sighed. "I wish with all my heart she would embrace the new religion, but she won't. She's as stubborn in her own way as old King Harry was in his."

Jane was shocked. "Surely you shouldn't speak of his grace, your father, so disrespectfully!"

"I mean him no disrespect, Jane, and I'm certain he would know it. Never have I loved or esteemed a man more than him." Suddenly Edward brightened. "Will you be there to watch

77

me tomorrow at the tournament? It will be my first!"

"Marry, your grace, of course I will." And to watch your cousin Edward as well, Jane added to herself with a secret smile. He would be wearing a token she had made him herself. A small, embroidered silken square, folded and tucked beneath the plume of his helmet.

The Christmas tournament took place under skies uncharacteristically warm and sunny for December. Jane sat on the balcony of Whitehall Palace and watched the parade of colours pass by beneath her. Her heart gave a queer bump and missed a beat as Lord Edward, Earl of Hertford, looked her way and bowed to her. There was a stir amongst her ladies, and stifled giggles. Jane smiled and waved back to him. Then her smile faded as she saw the Lord Admiral scowling at her. He was also on the field and had seen the exchange. Jane scowled back at him. The man must be mad. Surely he had given up any wild notions of marrying her to the king. The king must marry a princess of royal blood, he had said so himself. Her attention was diverted as a roar from the crowd told her the jousting was about to begin.

The king himself was to start the tournament off. He was matched against a boy his own age — Lord Arundel's son. The two boys faced each other at opposite ends of the field, then spurred their horses furiously on, lances lowered. It seemed that Edward's lance barely brushed his opponent's shield, then the boy was unhorsed and lying on the ground. Edward looked displeased and removed his helmet. Jane wondered if he knew he had been allowed to win.

It seemed he did.

"The king's majesty does not expect to win constantly," he announced in ringing tones. He glared at the remaining combatants. "Sometimes it is God's will for even a prince to be bested, that we should lose to teach us Christian humility."

Obligingly, his cousin Edward, who was the next contestant, knocked him off his horse with a solid *thwang*. The crowd gasped. Jane gasped with them, torn between pride at the young Earl of Hertford's skill and dismay at his daring.

Edward allowed himself to be helped up, laughing, and the crowd relaxed.

"I hope, however, I am not to be taught *too* much humility today," he announced ruefully.

"Your noble father, the king's grace, was never defeated at jousting," Arundel's son remarked loudly and somewhat acidly. Apparently his own easy defeat was rankling.

Again the crowd gasped and held their breaths at his audacity. Edward, however, seemed to be in a singularly good mood and able to forgive even this effrontery.

"Our noble father, God rest his soul, was never defeated at *anything* when he was in the prime of his life," he said. "And neither, with God's help, shall I be."

So much for humility, thought Jane wryly.

Jane watched the rest of the tournament with amusement until she saw them bring out a live goose and hang it upside down by its feet from a post. Then she rose and hastily excused herself. She knew what was coming. This particular bout was one which she had watched once and vowed never to watch again. The goose was greased, and the winner was the one who could gallop past, reach out, and rip the slippery head off.

She made her way back inside the palace and headed for an alcove in the long gallery where she could rest until the tournament had finished. It was a favourite spot of hers, slightly private and away from things, and it was a place where she often went when the king was busy and could not see her. To her surprise there was a figure sitting there already. He rose as she approached. It was the young Earl of Hertford, changed out of his tournament apparel.

"Lord Edward!" Jane exclaimed, surprised. "Are you finished competing in the tournament?"

"I have no more liking for this event than do you, my lady, and I thought I might find you here. Will you join me for a while? It's not often we have the opportunity to be alone."

"With pleasure," Jane replied. She sat down on the velvet window cushion and he took his place beside her.

They talked for a while of the tournament, of court affairs, of harmless gossip. Then Edward suddenly became serious. "My lady," he said. "I know it is early to speak of such matters, but there is something that has been on my mind much of late. May I speak of it to you?"

"Of course," Jane answered, her heart beating a little more rapidly.

"My lord father has spoken to me of my

future marriage," Edward said. Usually light-hearted and full of confidence, he suddenly seemed shy. "He feels — he feels that an alliance between our two families would be very appropriate." Edward was looking at the carpet beneath his feet, one foot carefully tracing out its pattern. "Do you — do you think you might agree?"

Jane looked at his downturned face with a twinkle in her eye. She wasn't nearly as shy as he, but it would never do to let him see that.

"I think — I think I most certainly agree," she answered demurely. She lowered her eyelids just in time to avoid letting him see the delight in her eyes.

"Then if my father approached your father . . ." Edward was looking at Jane eagerly. "Would he consent?"

At this the twinkle went out. *Would* he consent? That was the problem. Would her mother let him? It was an excellent match, most suitable. But were they still hoping? Still plotting? And the Lord High Admiral was her guardian. What would he have to say about the match?

Her troubled look bothered Edward.

"What is it? Is there some obstacle? Surely you are not already promised?"

"No. It's just that my father — I don't know what plans he has for me, what he will say."

"He has not promised you to my uncle, the Lord Admiral?" Edward exploded. "I've heard the admiral is desperate to marry royalty, but neither of the princesses will have anything to do with him."

"Heaven forbid!" Jane cried. "The admiral has no wish to marry me!" But in spite of herself, her mind began turning over this new possibility. If, indeed, he had failed at his plan for marrying her to the king, and at marrying one of the princesses himself, could he be thinking of marrying her? Her mother was royal and closely connected to the throne. "I would die sooner than marry him! I detest that man!"

"No more than do I," Edward answered grimly. "I cannot see why our cousin, the king's grace, has such affection for him." He turned to face Jane fully and took one of her hands in his. "But let's not talk about my uncle. It's an unpleasant subject." He seemed about to add more, but a sudden surge of noise and inrush of people told them that the last event was over. Reluctantly, Edward dropped Jane's hand and they rose to join the rest.

*   *   *

By January, however, the Lord High Admiral was beginning to act strangely. His merry, light-hearted manner became more forced, and at times he lashed out with an uncharacteristic anger. His plans for marrying Jane to the king were obviously not succeeding, and even the king was beginning to doubt him.

"He is trying to turn me against the Duke of Somerset, Jane," Edward told her one day. "I know the Lord Protector is a harsh man, and I have often complained about him myself, but I cannot believe the things my uncle is saying against him. And there is a look about the admiral these days, almost of desperation. I think he wants the power my other uncle has so badly that he will stop at nothing to get it. I'm almost afraid of him, Jane."

Jane, indeed, was beginning to be very afraid of him. She tried to avoid his presence at all times, especially when he came raging into the house, furious with some imagined slight or offence offered to him by his brother. His rages became more and more frequent, however, until little could be seen of his former good humour. Finally his behaviour turned the king against him to such an extent that Edward refused to receive him. This, in turn, enraged the admiral to the point where he seemed almost to lose his sanity.

"I must see the king!" he roared at Jane late one afternoon when she had been unable to avoid meeting him upon his return from another futile try for an audience with Edward. "He must see me! I will force him to make my brother listen to me, share his responsibilities with me."

"*Force* him, my lord?" Jane asked, aghast. "You speak of *forcing* his grace, the king?"

"Yes. If necessary. The king's grace must see that my brother is keeping him from me. Filling his mind with lies and false scandals. Poisoning him against me." He reached for his pistol and threw it on the table in front of him. "Yes, I will force him, if necessary. And here is the means to do it!"

Jane stared at him, terrified. There was a wild, mad look to him.

"Come, Jane," he suddenly ordered,

brusquely. "You will go with me to the palace. Your dear cousin sees you whenever you wish. You will gain an audience for me with him."

"But, my lord, his grace will not — he has stated that he will not see you. There's nothing I can do, my lord."

"We shall see. If you know what is good for you, my lady, you'll secure an audience for me. You are my ward, pray do not forget that fact. *You are in my charge and safekeeping.*" The threat implicit in the words was unmistakable.

Hardly bothering with the pretense of courtesy, he hurried Jane before him down the water steps to the waiting barge.

By the time they reached Whitehall, the king had retired. When he heard Jane wished to see him, however, he sent word that she was to be conducted to his bedchamber immediately.

"What is it, cousin? You look terrified!" The king was sitting before the fire, his dog, as usual, at his feet.

"It's my lord, the admiral," Jane answered, hardly able to force the words out. "He insists on seeing you. He has forced me to come to you to ask you to see him. Oh, cousin, I think he is mad!"

Hardly had she spoken when there was a commotion at the door and the admiral himself burst in. His face was scarlet and his eyes were wild.

"You *will* see me!" he cried. "You *will* hear me out!"

Several footmen made as if to throw themselves on the distraught man, but at that instant the king's tiny dog sprang to its feet and, growling as ferociously as it could manage, lunged for the admiral with fangs bared. With a muffled curse, the admiral pulled out his pistol. The shot rang out just as the footmen overpowered him and wrestled him to the ground. The little dog collapsed.

Jane, unable to move with shock, stared at the pool of blood seeping from the small corpse. Edward, too, stood frozen. Then he let out a cry of rage and anger.

"You will pay for this, Uncle! You will pay!"

7

Treason

"Guards! Guards! To the king! To the king!"

The cry rang out as loudly as had the shot, the echoes of which still reverberated in Jane's ears. She watched, stunned, as the halberdiers surrounded the admiral and dragged him roughly away. Then she turned to Edward. He was bent over the lifeless form of his dog, weeping. She knew he would not wish her to see him thus, so she turned away quickly. Slowly her mind began to work again. What would happen now? What was she to do? Return to her parents as soon as possible, obviously, but they were still at Bradgate.

The tapestries in the doorway were drawn back and a man dressed all in black strode in. He stared around him, taking in the scene with cold, calculating eyes. Jane drew in her breath as she recognized John Dudley, the Earl of Warwick. Instantly, the intense feeling of fear and dislike she had felt towards him at the coronation returned. His gaze travelled past Edward and settled on her. His eyebrows arched.

"My lady," he said, acknowledging her presence with the briefest of nods before setting his chin again in its usual arrogant tilt. Then he spoke to Edward, never, however, taking his eyes off Jane's face.

"His grace, the Duke of Somerset, has been sent for, your majesty. He will be here directly. You will wish to return to Seymour Place, Lady Jane," he added. It was not a question. "I will also arrange for Lord Dorset to be notified as soon as possible, my lady. For the present, until matters are more suitably arranged, you will no doubt wish to stay with Lady Seymour." Again there was no suggestion of a question in the tone of his voice.

Jane wondered at his easy assumption of authority in the absence of the Lord Protector. She was grateful that someone had taken the situation in hand, but was still so overwhelmed with distrust of the man that she couldn't bring herself to speak. She returned his nod with one equally brief.

Within the hour she was returned to Seymour Place. Here all was confusion. Lady Seymour had swooned immediately upon hearing the news of her son's actions, and she had been put to bed. The servants were running about like headless sheep — there was no sign of supper, no sense of order at all. Jane escaped to her rooms gratefully. There she found Mrs. Ellen and most of her ladies twittering in excitement. Jane brushed past them and into her own bedchamber, ignoring their questions and exclamations. Mrs. Ellen followed, and behind her, a trifle hesitantly, came young Elizabeth Tylney.

"Keep the others out, Mrs. Ellen, please do. I

cannot speak to anyone just now." She reached out for her old nurse's hand and held it tightly.

"Mistress Tylney," Mrs. Ellen said sharply, "do you go and arrange immediately for some hot food for her ladyship." She waved aside Jane's protesting hand. "Nonsense, my lady. You are as pale as death. You must take some nourishment after such a shock."

The girl ran from the room.

"What will they do to him?" Jane asked weakly. Much as she disliked the admiral, the thought of the consequences of his impetuousness was terrifying.

"If what I heard is true, he'll not keep that handsome head for very much longer, I should say. And well shall it serve him indeed. Attacking the king! Putting you in danger as well!"

"He didn't attack the king," Jane protested. "He just wanted to speak to him."

"Indeed!" The word was a snort. "And is that why he burst into the king's private chambers with a loaded pistol? The talk is that he meant to abduct his grace and force the good duke to give in to his demands. Imagine! Laying hands on the king's person!"

"But he didn't. He never touched him."

"Never you mind, love. He'll get what he deserves and we'll be away from here and well rid of him. Good riddance, I say."

Jane sank down onto the four-poster bed and stared up at the elaborately carved frame. Her mind was too full of the event she had just witnessed to be able to think coherently. All she could see was the little dog lying in a crumpled heap of red-matted fur. Slowly Mrs. Ellen's words sank in. She clung to them in relief. At least this meant that she would go home. Back to Bradgate. Back to a life of peace and sanity.

*   *   *

On the twentieth of March, 1549, Thomas Seymour, Lord High Admiral of England, was executed. His brother, the Duke of Somerset, signed the death warrant.

Shortly afterwards, as soon as the weather allowed, Jane and her parents returned to Bradgate. The roads were still muddy and the weather dismal, but not nearly as dismal as the tempers of Lord Dorset and Lady Frances. Their hopes for a marriage for Jane with King Edward lay in ruins. With one act, Thomas Seymour had shattered all their plans. Unreasonable as it seemed, they vented all their frustrations and anger on Jane. They had not spoken to her civilly since they arrived to fetch her, and unless she was careful of every word she spoke, she was apt to receive a scornful glare from one or the other, or even a blow. She had not been able to see the Protector's son before they left, but with the present state of her parents' temper, did not even dare to mention his name. The joy of returning to Bradgate, therefore, was tempered with gloom.

Jane's heart lifted, nevertheless, when the graceful red brick walls and towers of Bradgate Manor came into view. It looked exactly the same as when she had left. The two years that had changed her life so dramatically had made no difference here. To Jane, this was reassuring. This was one thing in her life that was constant.

Katherine and Mary were waiting to greet her in the winter parlour. Jane had seen very little of Katherine in the past two years, and nothing at all of Mary. Even as she was hugging and kissing them, and being hugged and kissed in return, it pained her to see now that Mary had hardly grown during that time, but seemed more misshapen, more dwarfish than ever. She gave her an extra loving squeeze, then they all ran together up to her beloved tower room.

It was just as she had left it.

"Oh, it's so *good* to be home!" she cried, hugging Katherine yet again and turning to sweep Mary into her arms as well, as the small child straggled into the room behind them.

But two weeks later the joy of returning had diminished somewhat. Her parents were strict with her to the point of cruelty. Although Jane had always been an excellent scholar, and continued to make progress with her beloved tutor, John Aylmer, they seemed to demand the impossible from her. No mistakes were allowed, no imperfections, no relief from constant study. This last did not bother Jane too much, as she honestly preferred the company of John Aylmer to that of her parents.

Her parents, in their turn, spent their time hunting, making merry, and gambling. Jane, who was used to the ordered, intellectual life she had lived with Katherine Parr, disapproved of them strongly, their gambling in particular. In the increasingly strict Protestantism that was taking over England, gambling was severely frowned upon. In this matter Jane was supported by Dr. Haddon, the family chaplain, but he did not dare speak out against the formidable Lady Frances. Jane had no such fears, however. Her two years away from her family had taught her an independence and self-confidence she had not known before. She criticized her parents to their faces, demanded that they adhere to the rules of the new religion they professed to follow. They, of course, resented her puritanical preaching and found even more offences for which to punish her.

Matters came to a head one evening when Jane was called to attend her parents in the winter parlour. She entered cautiously, not knowing what to expect, what kind of mood they would be in.

Lord Dorset and Lady Frances were at cards with several of their friends, their faces flushed, their eyes unnaturally bright. Jane's lips set in a grim line of disapproval.

"Well, milady," Lady Frances said, her words slurring slightly, "we've called you to recite for us. Show our dear friends some of the *vast* amount of learning for which you are so renowned." The words were irritating and insulting, and meant to be so.

Jane bridled immediately. "An it please my lady mother, I am very occupied at the moment and would prefer to return to my studies."

There was a general intake of breath. Lady Frances half rose out of her seat, stumbled, then sank back down.

"It would seem the greatest thing you have learned, milady, is impertinence!" Her small, beady eyes were almost bulging out of her head, and she seemed to be having trouble breathing.

Jane's father jumped up and advanced on her threateningly. "You will do as your lady mother requests!" he ordered. One hand was lifted as if to strike, even in the presence of company.

Jane flinched involuntarily, then straightened her back. In a dead monotone, as quickly as she could, she began to recite the passage of Plato she had been working on that morning. In Latin. The assembled guests shifted uncomfortably. It wasn't long until their eyes glazed over with boredom and they squirmed even more restlessly. With perverse satisfaction, Jane droned on. She was even beginning to enjoy herself. On and on she went, until even her parents began to be noticeably ill at ease.

Finally her mother was forced to raise her hand. "That is enough. You may go now." She spoke haughtily with an attempt at dignity, but Jane had won this round and Lady Frances knew it.

The victory cost Jane dearly, however. When she finally retired to bed that night, she had to lie carefully on her side to avoid the pain of several red welts on her back.

*   *.   *

Gradually, however, a new development began to disrupt the familiar routines of Bradgate. Messengers from London and other parts of the country began to appear more and more frequently at the gates. Jane began to hear stories of general discontent in the land — uprisings and rebellion. It seemed there were two main causes for this. One was the continued enclosure of land by the great lords for their own use, land which the common people had always considered public. The other centred on the further changes being made in the established religion.

The people were confused and upset by those changes. Priests were now allowed to marry. Mass was forbidden. The Communion service was altered, its very nature changed to a point that was unacceptable to many. No longer were they allowed to believe that transmutation occurred during the holy service so that the bread and wine they consumed were the actual body and blood of Christ their Saviour. Now they were to accept the bread and wine as symbols only of His body and blood and the sacrifice He had made for them. Services were held in English instead of Latin, and worst of all to many, the prayer book had been translated into English by Archbishop Cranmer.

At the height of all these rumours and unrests, a large party came riding up the road to Bradgate. Jane, from her tower window, was one of the first to spot it. She watched the cloud of dust and the horsemen curiously as they drew nearer, then her heart started to bound with a life all of its own as she recognized the standard of the Duke of Somerset. With such a large party, the duke must be coming himself! Would Edward be with him? She had had no news of him since her return.

"Mrs. Ellen!" she called. "Mrs. Ellen, come, do!"

The old nurse hurried in. Jane grabbed her by the wrist and squeezed so tightly the poor lady winced.

"Mrs. Ellen, send someone to find out who is with the duke's party. Why are they here? Is Lord Edward with them?" The words tumbled out so quickly they could hardly be understood.

"Now, now, my lady," Mrs. Ellen replied, imperturbable as ever. Then she turned. "Mistress Tylney," she called, "be you so good as to go and ascertain who is with the duke's party so our young mistress here will not perish of apoplexy." She was smiling as she gave the order, and Elizabeth Tylney smiled back as she winked at Jane over the nurse's shoulder.

Within minutes she was back with the news. Edward was indeed with the party. More surprising, the duchess herself was also with them, and Lady Frances was in a state. The Duchess of Somerset was one of the most unreasonable, demanding, haughty and difficult women ever created by God, Lord Dorset had often remarked, and most women and many men quailed before her. She was even more than a match for Lady Frances, and her arrival had thrown Jane's mother into a tizzy. The unexpected arrival of the duke's entire party had thrown the whole household into a tizzy.

Jane waited in her room with an impatience that was almost unbearable. Surely she would be called for. Surely she would be invited down to meet the guests! It was almost the hour of supper before the summons came, however. When the page appeared to call her, Jane dashed for the mirror to smooth her hair yet again, then raced to the door.

"Slow down, my lady! Calm yourself!"

Jane didn't even hear Mrs. Ellen's words; she tore down the stairs with the abandon of the child she no longer was. She did manage to pause and collect herself before entering the room, however. When the page ushered her in, only her sparkling eyes betrayed her excitement.

The Duke of Somerset was standing by the fire, the duchess sitting beside him. Lady Frances was officiously seeing to the serving of a plate of sweet cakes. Jane hardly looked at them before her eyes found Edward. He was standing slightly to one side. When he saw Jane he broke into a huge grin. By the time Jane had made her proper obeisances to the duke and duchess, he was at her side. They stood smiling at each other, neither one of them able to say a word.

It wasn't until much later, after the supper, that Jane had a chance to talk to Edward alone. They had left the others to their conversation and escaped gratefully to the garden. Now they exploded with talk.

"I wondered so how you were!" Jane exclaimed.

"No more than I. London is dreary without you. The king himself says he misses you and wishes you were there."

"How is he? I wish I could see him again!"

"He is well. Negotiations are under way for a marriage with the Princess of France, and he is taking on more and more duties himself — somewhat to my dear father's discomfiture, I sometimes think," Edward added with a smile. "Progressing rapidly in his mastery of the bow and in all other manner of sports, just as his royal father did, God rest his soul, and proud as a peacock of himself for it."

Jane returned his smile, remembering the king's words at his first tournament. Humility, it seemed, was not to be one of his virtues.

"But, my lord," Jane asked suddenly, "what is the purpose of your visit? What brings the good duke here?"

"Two reasons," Edward answered. "The first is not so interesting. He wants your father's help in subduing any signs of unrest here in Leicestershire. The revolts are growing more and more grave and they must be put down immediately." For a moment his young face was serious, then it lightened. "The second reason is why my lady mother and I are with him, and it is by far the most interesting and important reason as far as I am concerned." He stopped and waited for Jane's response, looking at her gleefully.

"What? What is it? Oh, don't tease me! What is it?"

"Why, it is to arrange our betrothal, my lady. What else could it be?"

Jane's eyes widened as she stared at him in disbelief, then she suddenly blushed and lowered them in confusion. "Is this true, my lord? You are not jesting?"

Edward reached for her hand quickly. "You know I would not jest about this, my lady. My lord father believes this would be an excellent match, and my lady mother, thank heaven, agrees. I imagine they are all discussing it at this very moment."

Jane's mind began to work quickly. Edward had mentioned a possible match for the king with the Princess of France. If this were so, then there would be no reason for her parents to object. Indeed, they would be lucky to be able to make such a good match. They couldn't possibly not agree. They must consent!

And they did. Jane and Edward were informed of their decision the next day, just before the duke's party left. To Jane and Edward, their time together had been very short, but at least there were promises of seeing each other again soon when she and her family returned to their London house at the end of summer.

* * *

Events conspired to frustrate this, however. The revolts and uprisings became more violent and widespread. Finally, by July, martial law had been declared and public hangings were taking place in London. Sir Thomas Wyatt had managed to put down the revolt in Kent, but the name that Jane kept hearing more and more was that of the Earl of Warwick, the dark man whom she had feared and disliked so much at King Edward's coronation. Letters she received from Edward mentioned him frequently, never in a positive vein. Edward seemed to distrust the man as much as Jane did.

"He is weaselling his way into the king's

affections," he wrote. "Obviously trying to take the place of my uncle, the Lord High Admiral, God rest his soul. Indeed, there are rumours he was instrumental in convincing King Edward and my father that my uncle should be put to death. Now, I fear, he is turning the minds of the other lords in the Privy Council against my father. He is an ambitious man."

Jane remembered the description she had heard of him the first time she had seen him: "a man of vaulting ambition." She shuddered. Surely he could not harm the Duke of Somerset, however. The good duke was the most powerful man in England, next to the king himself.

By August the country had begun to settle back down. One way or another, by force or persuasion, people were beginning — outwardly at least — to accept the new ways. The Earl of Warwick had succeeded in putting down the rebellion in East Anglia. His name was on everyone's lips by now, and his fame as a soldier was beginning to spread. But even those who praised him did so cautiously. His cold and calculating manner inspired reluctant admiration rather than affection from the people, and many were distrustful of his motives.

The Duke of Somerset wrote to congratulate Lord Dorset on his success in restoring his county to peace and quiet, and thanked him particularly for his constant and good diligence in the king's service.

Lord Dorset preened himself on the letter. "I think we should plan to return to Dorset House next month, my lady wife," he remarked to Lady

Frances. "I expect our little lady here would like to see her betrothed again as well," he added with an uncharacteristically good-humoured smile in Jane's direction.

Jane smiled back, for once in total agreement with her father. "I would indeed," she answered.

They left in late September and arrived in London the second week in October after a leisurely journey, with many stops and much visiting with relatives and friends along the way. This time Jane enjoyed the trip immensely. The fields were brimming with grain; the weather was sunny and pleasant. Magpies flashed in and out of the trees; the roads themselves were alive with packmen, peddlars, and travelling caravans. They even passed a troupe of showmen hastening to exhibit a dancing bear and some trained dogs and pigs at a neighbouring fair. Jane laughed along with the others as the troupe was persuaded to give an impromptu show for them.

Both Katherine and Mary were accompanying her this time, and this added to her pleasure. "Life could not be better, sweet sisters, could it?" Jane asked as the spires of London finally came into view.

There was a strange air to the city as they rode in, however. The streets were even more thronged with people, but the usual rowdy calling and hoots of laughter were missing. People hurried to and fro with a worried, almost furtive attitude.

Lord Dorset and his party grew more and more curious the farther they rode. Finally Lord Dorset reined in his horse and shouted to a passing clerk. "Good my man, do you come here for a moment."

When the apprehensive young man stood beside him, Jane's father looked down at him. "What has happened, my good man? What is the matter with all these people?"

"Why, have you not heard, my lord?" was the astonished reply. "The Duke of Somerset, our own good duke, has been seized and thrown into the Tower. He is accused of treason and plotting against his grace, the king!"

8

Ill-fated betrothal

Jane stared at the man, incredulous. The Duke of Somerset? Edward's father? It was impossible!

Her father looked as thunderstruck as she felt. For a moment he was speechless, and in that moment the clerk darted away. Lord Dorset looked as if he might hail some other passerby, then suddenly changed his mind.

"Clear the way!" he shouted to the servants ahead of them. "Make haste and clear the way, I say!" He galloped forward, scattering people to right and left of him. The rest of his party were left to follow as best they could.

As soon as he arrived at Dorset House, Lord Dorset threw his reins to a waiting groom. "Have a fresh beast ready for me immediately. I'll ride to the palace within the hour."

Within much less than an hour, Jane heard the striking of hooves on the cobblestones and ran to her window just in time to see her father riding furiously out of the courtyard. Until he returned she would have to simmer with impatience — the servants at Dorset House knew no more about the matter than had the clerk on the street.

Jane paced the narrow confines of the room she shared with Katherine, waiting to hear the clatter of returning hooves. Katherine had sat up with her for a while, but had soon tired and was now asleep. There could be no sleep for Jane, however, until she had learned more. What charges could they possibly have trumped up against the good duke? She remembered Edward's forebodings and was certain that the Earl of Warwick was behind it.

It was far into the night before her father returned. As soon as she heard his horse, Jane grabbed for a shawl and ran down the stairs. Much to Mrs. Ellen's consternation, she had refused to undress that evening, so she was still fully clothed. She reached the winter parlour, where her mother was waiting, just as Lord Dorset strode in.

"Jane, what are you doing here? Return to your room at once, child," her mother began, but Lord Dorset interrupted her and took no notice of Jane at all.

"This is a nice mess indeed," he exploded as he stormed into the room, tossing cape and gauntlets into the rushes on the floor behind him. A manservant hastened to pick them up, then retreated fearfully as Lord Dorset ranted on.

"A fine time we picked to announce the betrothal of our daughter to Somerset's son! By God's bones, every eye was upon me as I entered the palace, and there were many who were sneering with delight, I'll tell you!"

"But the duke, father! What possible charges —"

"Faugh! The duke's as big a fool as his brother was. Do you know what that madman did? He'd got the lords all stirred up against him with his mollycoddling of the people — disparking Hampton Court indeed! — then he tried to force them to go along with him by making off to Windsor with the king himself. Virtually kidnapped him in order to get his way and to assure his own safety against the wrath of the other lords!"

"I always said he was mad," Lady Frances burst out. "He and that terrible wife of his. I knew no good would come of an alliance with them."

Jane stared at her, remembering the fawning and flattery she had heaped on the Duke and Duchess of Somerset during their visit to Bradgate. The corners of Jane's mouth curled down with disgust, but she had no time for her mother just then.

"What happened, father?" she asked impatiently.

"Why, the fool had only taken a small band of guards with him, so the lords came in force and routed him out, of course. It was all over with in one evening, and now the good duke is securely in the Tower where he'll either rot or die, I'll wager."

"Surely the king will not allow that. He loves his uncle deeply!" Jane couldn't imagine her cousin turning against his uncle under any circumstances.

"No more so than he loved his other uncle, until he proved false as well," her father retorted.

A sudden chill took hold of Jane's heart. Perhaps it was not so impossible after all. "And Lord Edward? What has become of him?" She was almost afraid to ask.

"What indeed? What are we to do now? You are betrothed to the son of a traitor!"

"I knew it was a mistake! I told you the match was not suitable!" Lady Frances towered over her husband in her anger.

"What has happened to Edward? Where is he?" Jane was almost frantic.

"I little know and care less. The shame of this, Jane! Do you realize the shame you have brought on this family?"

Jane turned and ran from the room. If her father didn't know what had happened to Edward, it probably meant that he was safe — at least for the time being. That was all she could think of for the moment.

Two days later, however, even that slight amount of relief was taken from her. Jane's suspicions of the Earl of Warwick seemed to be proving themselves valid. The Earl himself went to bring the king back to Hampton Court, and now seemed firmly in control of the situation. To Jane's dismay, hard upon that came the news that Lord Edward had been sent to France as hostage for his father's compliance.

"Hostage?" Jane demanded of her father when he told them of this latest development. "Of what possible use could Edward be as hostage?"

"It seems the Earl of Warwick has plans," Lord Dorset answered, "and needs the duke's co-operation. What better way to secure a man's co-operation than through the withholding of something that is precious to him? Indeed, wasn't that the duke's game as well when he kidnapped the king? He has just been outfoxed by a more clever player, that's all."

"A more unscrupulous and evil player, you mean," Jane muttered. Fortunately her father did not hear her.

"You must seek an audience with the Earl of Warwick immediately," Lady Frances broke in. "He must be assured of our loyalty in spite of this unfortunate alliance."

"I have already done so, my lady wife," Lord Dorset replied smoothly, "and as always, I have found him to be a most compatible person. We understand each other perfectly."

The chill that had taken hold of Jane's heart deepened. No good would come to her or to Edward through this suspicious union, of that she was certain.

*   *   *

Rumours flew back and forth, each one contradicting the last. The duke was to be tried. The duke was to be set free. The duke was accused of treason. The duke was not accused of anything. Jane was desperate to secure an audience with her cousin, the king, but for the time being he was seeing no one but the members of the Privy Council — John Dudley, the Earl of Warwick, in particular. Finally, however, he sent for her.

Jane rushed through the elaborate preparations necessary to make her presentable to the king as quickly as she could, despite the shocked

105

protestations of Mrs. Ellen, and presented herself at the palace within the hour. There, however, for the first time, she was kept waiting for almost another hour. She fidgeted and fretted until, by the time the footman finally came to fetch her to the king, she was almost beside herself.

"Cousin!" she cried even as she was rising from her first curtsy. "How could you? Your uncle whom you love so dearly! What will you do with him?"

Luckily the king was alone and there was no one to hear this outburst. Even so, Edward's face clouded and he glared at Jane as he had never done before.

"My lady, you forget yourself!" he said sharply.

"But, your grace, surely your good uncle meant you no harm —" Jane checked herself as she saw the look on Edward's face. Coming to her senses, she immediately swept into another low curtsy. "Forgive me, your grace. I speak too wildly. It is just . . ." She looked up at him appealingly. "What will happen to him?" she asked again. Then, barely in a whisper, "What will happen to Edward?"

At these words, the king's features softened and he held out his hand.

"Rise, Jane. We can understand why you are so distraught. Rest assured, nothing will happen to our good friend and yours, the Earl of Hertford. But as to his father, our uncle" — his face clouded over again — "the Earl of Warwick has advised us —"

"Surely you won't listen to him!" Jane burst out, forgetting herself once more. "I distrust him, cousin. He means no good to any of us except himself, I'm certain of it!"

"Jane!"

At this further reproof, Jane flushed and bit her lip. She would have to control herself.

"The Earl of Warwick has been invaluable to us. We esteem his advice highly and will hear no complaints of him." Edward announced this stiffly and coldly, obviously annoyed with Jane all over again.

"I'm sorry, your grace. My words were ill-advised." Jane spoke humbly, but inside, her heart was raging.

Edward continued, suddenly becoming more friendly, her cousin again. "It was he who came to rescue me, Jane. Truly, I think my uncle was a little mad that night. My other uncle was too, you remember?" He looked at Jane anxiously.

She nodded, not trusting herself to speak.

"The Duke of Somerset roused me out of bed and spirited me away to Windsor in the dead of the night, without a word of explanation, Jane. Then when the lords came to rescue me with their troops, he forced me to stand at the portals and face them all beside him. There were so many of them! Spears clashing, torches flaring, such noise and confusion! I didn't know what was going to happen." Edward stopped. His face told Jane what he could never admit — how frightened he must have been. It would take a lot to make him forgive this uncle now.

Pages entered bearing refreshments. Henry

Sidney and Barnaby Fitzpatrick frolicked in behind them and seemed bent on teasing and amusing their friend and king back to his normal, cheerful frame of mind, so Jane had no opportunity to question him further. The interview had done nothing to quell her fears, given her nothing to hope for at all.

*   *   *

The Christmas season was fast upon them. For Jane, it was a torment. The merrymaking and careless pleasure of the king and all those around him only served to increase her desperation. The duke remained in the Tower; Edward remained in France.

Then one sullen, gloomy day in February, a maidservant interrupted Jane at her studies with John Aylmer. "There is someone to see you, my lady," she announced, curtsying.

Jane looked up curiously. "Who is it?" she demanded.

"It's a young gentleman, my lady. He won't give his name and demands to see you at once."

Jane stood up. She knew no young gentleman who would come calling specifically to see her. Her parents were both out — perhaps it was someone to see them and the maidservant had become confused. Excusing herself from her tutor, she followed the girl back downstairs, her mind still half on the lesson she had been doing. By the screens in the great hall she stopped. There, waiting for her, was Edward.

"Jane!" he cried.

In the joy of the moment, all formality was

forgotten. They ran forward, then stopped, suddenly shy, a short distance away from each other.

"How is this possible? I heard nothing of your return. Even my lord father heard nothing. What has happened? Has your lord father been released?" The questions and exclamations flew out of Jane's mouth, one on top of another.

Edward laughed. "All is well, my lady." He stopped, then continued a little less lightheartedly. "Or, at least, almost well. My father has been released and I am brought back here to stay."

"Oh, Edward." In spite of the cold drizzle outside, Jane felt the whole warmth of a summer sun flooding through her. "I worried — I hoped —" She shook her head to clear her eyes of the tears that suddenly flooded them. "But you said 'almost well,' " she added quickly, picking up the hesitant words. "What has happened? Come, sit here and tell me all." She drew him into the parlour where a fire was blazing cheerily, and pulled him down to a seat beside her. "Tell!" she commanded, forgetting to let go of his hand.

"My father has been released," Edward repeated, "but there was a price. He will no longer be Lord Protector, but will be allowed to return to the Privy Council."

"Who then will be Protector?"

"They say no one, that all the Council will be equally responsible for the king and the kingdom. But in fact that is not quite so. There is one who will be more powerful, even though none dare admit it."

"The Earl of Warwick," Jane stated, her voice grim.

"Exactly," Edward replied. "And it is he who has dictated the terms of my father's release."

"And they are?"

"Most of his lands confiscated to the king. Most of our possessions handed over. Great wealth is no longer ours, Jane. Indeed, very little wealth remains to us at all. What will your parents do now?"

"What can they do? We are promised. They cannot break a promised betrothal!" Jane spoke defiantly, but in her heart she was not so sure. Her parents had a habit of doing exactly as they willed.

"There is more," Edward went on. "My sister, Lady Anne, is to be married to Lord Lisle, the Earl's eldest son. I suppose in this way he will maintain his power over us. And the Earl's daughter, Lady Mary, is to be married to our cousin Edward's good friend, Lord Henry Sidney. The Earl of Warwick is entrenching himself marvellously."

They both fell silent for a moment. The future loomed uncertainly ahead of them.

Then Jane straightened herself up resolutely. "Never mind. You are back. Your father is released and restored to a measure of power. We are still betrothed. Oh, Edward, it could have been so much worse!"

Edward relaxed and smiled as well. "Yes, you are right. It could have. We must grasp what we can and be happy with it."

*   *   *

And so, for the next year, they did. Lord Dorset and Lady Frances were obviously not pleased with the situation, but there was little they could do to change it at this time. As long as the Duke of Somerset remained in favour and in limited power, there was no way they could refute the betrothal. In October Jane would celebrate her fourteenth birthday. She would be of marriageable age, Edward was two years older — there was no reason why the wedding should not be planned forthwith. Jane began to argue for it, breaking her parents' resistance down bit by bit.

Then an event happened which changed the situation considerably. Jane's grandfather, the old Duke of Suffolk, had died, leaving the dukedom to his eldest son, the Lady Frances's young half-brother. In the summer of this year, however, both this boy and his younger brother had succumbed to the sweating sickness that was raging throughout the city, and died. In this manner Lady Frances inherited the title Duchess of Suffolk, and Lord Dorset assumed the title of Duke. This unexpected and exalted rise in their fortunes was eagerly seized by the grasping pair. In no time at all they had moved themselves and their daughters into a royal suite at Richmond Palace, and their attitude towards the king, while still respectful, became far more intimate.

"They are thinking of that marriage again, I'm certain of it," Jane exclaimed to Mrs. Ellen. "I can see it in my lady mother's eyes whenever she looks at me and the king together. Her ambitions are overreaching themselves again, and I'm afraid of what it will do to Lord Edward and myself!"

"But, my lady, surely they will not break their word?" The soft, comforting voice of Elizabeth Tylney broke in. As soon as Jane had been installed at Richmond she had sent for the girl again. They had become good friends during the time Jane had spent with the Lord High Admiral, and Jane had missed her since then, even though she had the company of her own sisters.

"I'm afraid, Mistress Tylney, my mother stops at nothing to get what she wants."

The new Duchess of Suffolk was destined to be thwarted in this design, however, as hard upon their removal to Richmond Palace, the betrothal of King Edward to Princess Elizabeth of France was formally announced.

Jane rejoiced at the news and rejoiced at the barely concealed, bitter disappointment of her parents. Her betrothal was safe again, and she began to bedevil them in earnest.

Court activities took on a much greater importance now, with their own greater prominence. Jane chafed at the time-wasting rituals, preferring to be left to her books and the visits of her beloved Edward, but she was forced to participate in spite of herself. Her mother was determined to take her rightful place at court, where her only rival now was the detested Duchess of Somerset. And how *that* galled her! She was equally determined that Jane and, to a lesser degree, Katherine should take their places beside her. Mary only was excused, and this because her mother was secretly ashamed of her appearance, Jane believed. Jane, of course, only loved her little sister all the more because of this, and tried to spend even more time with her.

In the autumn of 1551 Mary of Guise, the Queen Dowager and Regent of Scotland, requested leave to pass through England on her way back from France. She had been visiting her daughter Mary, the young Queen of Scotland, who was betrothed to the Dauphin of France and being brought up at the French court. King Edward graciously gave his permission and resolved to receive her in royal fashion.

The court immediately was thrown into a frenzy of preparations for the reception and banquet to be given in her honour. The Duchess of Suffolk prepared to outdo herself — *and* the Duchess of Somerset, it went without saying. Her chambers overflowed with silks and velvets. Seamstresses buzzed around like excited bees as she created an appropriate costume for herself.

Jane was also to make her first formal appearance at court under her new status, but she refused to take part in the dressmaking chaos. "This finery and elaborate overdressing ill becomes me, my lady mother," she protested. "And indeed, does not the good Dr. Latimer preach against the vanity and pomp of heathenish decoration of oneself as well as of churches?"

Protestantism was dictating simple, restrained manners in dress, and Jane had converted to its dictates with alacrity. In this she took as her model the Princess Elizabeth. The princess, although she preferred to remain on her own estates away from court life, was known to have adopted a quiet, even severe form of dress.

The week before the arrival of the Queen Dowager of Scotland, however, a box arrived for Jane from the Princess Mary. Mary also stayed away from London most of the time, but in her case it was because Mass was now forbidden to be celebrated there. Only in the privacy of her own manor could she practise her Catholic religion, and even this was beginning to be a difficult situation. The Princess Mary was still a good friend to the duchess, however, and presents flew back and forth between them unceasingly. This time it was a dress of finest scarlet silk with an overdress of rich silver brocade for Jane. Jane hated it on sight.

"Surely I will not insult her grace, the Princess Elizabeth, by straying so far from her example as to wear *this!*" she cried. "Return it to the Princess Mary," she told the footman who had presented it to her. "Thank her for me most graciously, but convey my regrets that the dictates of my conscience and my religion do not permit me such frippery."

"*Stay!*" roared the duchess. "You will do no such thing! You will bear the Lady Jane's most express gratitude and humble delight to her highness, and assure her that she will take immense pleasure in the wearing of such a splendid gift."

The poor footman, panic-stricken, hastened to leave the room as quickly as possible.

Jane set her mouth and glared at her mother. "I will not wear that."

"You will."

The duchess had her way, as usual. Jane appeared at her side to welcome the Queen Dowager arrayed as splendidly and as brilliantly as her mother. Her face was pale and her whole complexion jarred with the garish colour. Around her throat glittered the Princess Mary's other gift to her — a necklet of tiny, deep red rubies. As Jane made her entrance into the grand ballroom of Westminster Palace, the jewels sparkled and glistened around her small neck like a circle of shimmering drops of blood.

Her mother beamed and smiled with complaisant approval.

9
Forebodings

"Have you heard the news, my lady? The Earl of Warwick is to be created Duke of Northumberland!" Elizabeth Tylney burst into Jane's bedchamber, almost breathless with excitement.

"But he can't be! He is not of royal blood! Only an Englishman with blood ties to the royal family can be made a duke." Jane looked at her young lady-in-waiting incredulously.

"Nevertheless it is true, my lady. They say the king is determined to reward him suitably for his services and he insists upon it."

Jane didn't answer, but her mind was whirling. John Dudley had been gaining more and more influence over the king with each passing day, she knew that, but she had had no idea just how much. If he could persuade the king to give him a dukedom, was there any limit to how far he could go?

It seemed there wasn't. One month later the news was released to shocked Londoners that the Duke of Somerset had once more been imprisoned. This time the charges were high treason and plotting to murder the Duke of Northumberland. There seemed to be little chance of the good duke escaping the executioner's axe.

As if to dissociate themselves completely from the whole affair, Jane's parents immediately launched themselves into a whirlwind of Christmas activities and swept Jane along with them. Without allowing her time to see or even communicate with Edward, they left with a company of almost two hundred horsemen to "do the rounds."

To begin with, they went to pay a visit to the Princess Mary. Jane's open disapproval of the princess's determination to keep to the old religion soon earned her first the dislike and then the hostility of the princess. Worry about the fate of the Duke of Somerset and of Edward were uppermost in Jane's mind, however, and she made no effort to be tactful or to appease Mary, in spite of the duchess's indignant urgings.

For Christmas they went to stay with relatives at Tylsey. It was an even worse Christmas for Jane than the one two years before when the Duke of Somerset had first been imprisoned. This time his execution was almost a certainty. How could Jane laugh with the others at the antics of the mummers, tumblers, and jugglers, delight in the nightingale-sweet voice of a young boy singer, or frolic and dance with the abandon of the other young people when at any moment the stroke of an axe could bring disaster? In fact, the stress and worry, combined with the rigours of constant travelling, were seriously affecting her health. She was obviously ill, but her parents

117

chose to dismiss this as mere weakness and stubbornness on her part and ignored it.

After Christmas they continued their journeyings. This time they travelled to Walden to stay with Lady Audley, sister of Jane's father. It was there, in late January, that a messenger brought the news from London.

"The good duke is dead!"

The message spread like wildfire around the manor house. Jane rushed immediately to the parlour, where her parents were interviewing the messenger.

"There was terrible panic and confusion at the end, your grace," he was gasping as Jane came in. He paused briefly to catch his breath.

"His grace, the duke, was standing on the scaffold making his last speech, when all of a sudden a whole party of soldiers came galloping at top speed up the hill. Welladay, of course everyone thought it was a reprieve. The king had changed his mind at the last minute and had sent a guard to release him! There was such shouting and rioting then as you never did see, your lordship. Some folk fell in the Tower moat, some were trampled underfoot, and at least four of 'em broke their necks in the scuffle. Oh, it was a great to-do!"

"What happened then? Why didn't they release him?" Jane asked, unable to contain herself any longer.

"Why, my lady, it wasn't a guard to release him at all. It was just the regular guard hurrying because they were arriving late, was all. When the people realized *that*, they turned right nasty, and more than a few noggins were cracked before the soldiers got them back under control."

"But the duke?" Jane insisted.

"The good duke just stood there as cool as you please during the whole scuffle. No one was paying him the least mind and he could have escaped ten times over, but he just stood his ground and waited for all to calm down, then went on with his speech. He's a gentleman, he is. Or was, I should say." At these last words his face fell and his whole body drooped.

"So he . . ."

"Yes, my lady. They killed him. The good Duke of Somerset is dead."

Jane turned and ran for her room. She threw herself down on the bed, heedless of Mrs. Ellen's worried fussing. The worst had happened. Edward's father was dead. The Duke of Northumberland was in full power now. Edward's fate, and therefore her own, lay in his hands. And what would that fate be? Something to suit the Duke of Northumberland's purposes, not theirs, of that she was certain. Her cheeks felt flushed and taut; her head pounded with pain. Gratefully, she felt Mrs. Ellen lay a cool cloth on her forehead and then, at the very end of her strength, she gave in to the fever and illness she had been fighting for so many weeks.

* * *

"The Duchess of Somerset has been imprisoned in the Tower, isn't that shocking?" Jane's mother was trying hard to look shocked, but not succeeding very well. A triumphant smile lurked

119

only too obviously around the corners of her mouth. She had now no other rival in England. The Duke of Northumberland might be the most powerful man at court, but the Duchess of Suffolk outranked the new Duchess of Northumberland, and they both knew it. "Poor Edward. He has been stripped of his rank and lands and made a ward of the king. No prospects at all now, of course." She barely glanced at Jane as she spoke.

"We are legally betrothed, my lady mother," Jane answered. She was still weak from her illness, but there was a steely note of determination in her voice nonetheless.

"We shall see about that, daughter," her mother answered. "I have had a letter from the Duke of Northumberland himself. He has some interesting ideas on the subject. He wishes us to return to London to discuss them further with him."

"*What* ideas? What can the duke have to do with my marriage?" A shade of panic crept into Jane's words despite all her efforts.

"You shall know when it is time for you to know," the duchess answered haughtily. "His grace, the duke, has kindly given us Sheen to stay in upon our return. He will be right across the river, at Syon House. It will be so convenient."

Jane's heart sank. It was beginning to sound more and more like a trap. She couldn't see what the trap was, but something was afoot, she was certain of it. Her mother was setting the bait, and she was the mouse. But a mouse had to be made to enter the trap before it was caught, and she wouldn't. They wouldn't catch her. They wouldn't!

They had returned to Bradgate after the news of the duke's execution — less because of Jane's illness than because it suited her parents' own plans — but now they made ready to leave it again. Jane quailed at the thought of yet another journey. She was nowhere near strong enough for it. And also, she found herself curiously loath to leave Bradgate, even though it meant returning to Edward. Something inside her seemed to whisper, "The last time. This is the last time you will see your home. The last time you will ride through this park."

The day before they were to leave, she saddled her mare and rode to the top of the barren hillside. At the summit, she didn't even bother to dismount, just sat quietly on the mare and looked around her. What a long time ago — five years it was — since she had sat here and seen the messenger coming up the road from London. The messenger bringing the summons that had changed her life so drastically. And now another summons had come from London. What changes would this one bring?

When they reached London, Jane sent a note to Edward. He came as soon as he received it, but Sheen was a long way upriver from the City of London, and to Jane it seemed like an interminable time before he arrived. The duchess received him with the barest possible amount of courtesy. Jane seethed with anger.

"It makes no matter, Jane," Edward said

quietly when they were allowed to withdraw to the small parlour. "So long as your parents do not break our betrothal, I care not how they treat me."

He looked tired and sad. Jane's heart went out to him.

"You are still a favourite of the king, Edward. Things will improve for you, I know they will. And my parents would not *dare* break our betrothal!" She wished she felt as certain as she sounded.

Edward managed a laugh. "You speak fiercely for a lady so small! I doubt that anyone would dare cross you. Even I shall be frightened of you when we are married."

"When we are married." Jane sighed. "And when will that be? My parents will not even discuss the date. And they are hatching something, I'm sure of it. There is something brewing. Something to do with the Duke of Northumberland. I'm afraid, Edward . . ." Her voice trailed off.

Suddenly she squared her shoulders and shook her head angrily as if to rid it of unwelcome thoughts. "But your lady mother, Edward," she continued, changing the subject abruptly. "How does she? Is she keeping well?"

"She is keeping well in health, but not in spirit, I'm afraid," Edward answered. "She is treated decently and has all her ladies with her, but life imprisoned in the Tower is not at all to her liking."

In spite of herself, Jane felt a small smile twitching into life. She could well imagine that life imprisoned in the Tower would not be to the liking of the haughty Duchess of Somerset. Edward caught her eye and grinned back. He knew his mother better than anyone. For a moment they were two light-hearted children again, sharing a secret joke, but the moment passed immediately.

"I must return to Westminster," Edward said.

"Oh, Edward. So soon? Can you not stay a while with me?"

"The king insisted that I return this even. He has not been himself lately — very irritable. I think he feels badly about my father, but there's something else. He does not seem well."

Jane looked at him with instinctive concern. The health of the king was of paramount importance.

"He is not sickening, Edward, surely? It's too early in the year for the sweating sickness."

"No, no. He's — he's just not himself."

But the king was sickening. Less than two weeks later he was in bed with what at first was reported to be smallpox, but later described as measles. Measles was bad enough, however. Often fatal, the disease left its victims weak and debilitated for months afterwards. As if to prove the lie to this, however, in June — only two months later — the king set out on a trip through the southern and western parts of his kingdom. He took his cousin, Lord Edward, the Earl of Hertford, with him, so it was with considerable delight and anticipation that Jane greeted her father's decision to embark on yet another series of visits of their own, culminating with a visit to the king's party in Oxford. Jane was completely recovered from her own illness by now and eager to go.

These months had been a time of uncertainty for Jane. Legally, she was still betrothed to Edward, but her parents refused to discuss the marriage or to make any plans for it. They parried all her questions with vague answers and hints of other, much more important plans. Meanwhile, they were becoming more and more intimate with the Duke of Northumberland.

To Jane's dismay, however, the visit with the king at Oxford did not go well. She was only able to see her betrothed very briefly, and her parents would not entertain him at all, let alone discuss the marriage. The king himself looked tired, and was just as irritable as Edward had described him a few months earlier. Jane did not dare risk annoying him further by bringing the matter to his attention. Most of the time was spent by Jane's parents closeted with the Duke of Northumberland. Jane's dismay was only increased by the smug look of satisfaction on her mother's face. By now she had decided that anything that pleased her mother was bound to displease her.

* * *

The king returned to London in time to celebrate his fifteenth birthday. He decided that Jane should celebrate hers with him, and a huge ball was planned. For a time it seemed as if King Edward had regained his health, and he joked and made merry with Jane and his friends as he had before. The night of the ball, he insisted on having Jane sit beside him all evening and share the honours with him. He was flushed, his eyes almost unnaturally bright, and he teased Jane unmercifully about the many young gallants who asked her to dance.

Jane relaxed and enjoyed the evening as she hadn't enjoyed anything for a long while. Forgotten, at least for the time being, were all her worries about her parents' plots and schemes. Edward was with her; despite the king's teasing and the heady attentions of the other young men, her eyes sought his constantly. They shared all the laughter and the amusement of the evening, together even when apart, just so long as they could see each other, catch each other's glance.

Suddenly there was a lull. The music paused, the voices dropped. Jane looked up. In through the doorway strode the Duke of Northumberland, followed by his five sons. They were all as tall as he, and equally imposing. The four eldest had their father's dark, almost swarthy colouring; the youngest was fair and of a slighter build. He was by far the handsomest of the brood, but there was a suggestion of weakness to the mouth, a hesitancy of bearing that Jane found instantly objectionable. She looked away, but not before he had glanced her way and caught her eye. He smiled. An ingratiating smile which Jane did not return. She shivered with an involuntary gesture of distaste for the whole family, then turned back to Edward and forgot all about the Dudleys.

At Christmas that year the festivities at court were more than usually elaborate. Jane suspected that all the gaiety and noise was meant to conceal the fact that the king, once again, was ill. It pained her to watch him making the effort to join in and appear to be enjoying himself.

"He looks so ill, Edward," she remarked one day in privacy to her betrothed. "Surely he should be resting, not making merry with all this crowd from morn to even."

"He will not admit to illness, Jane," Edward replied. "He refuses to allow anyone even to suggest that he is not well."

"But he is so thin. His face is so flushed and his eyes so bright. I have seen others wasting away like that, Edward. Others who did not get better."

Edward looked as worried as she. "No one can tell him what to do, Jane. You know that. No one except the Duke of Northumberland, of course, and he only encourages him to carry on doing as much as possible."

"The Duke of Northumberland!" Jane's voice was bitter. "It's not our king's welfare he has at heart, I vow."

"Hush, Jane!" Edward looked around quickly. "You must not speak so carelessly. Whatever the duke has in his heart, the king dotes on him and depends on him for everything. He will hear no evil talk about him. Indeed, he is almost unreasonable on the subject. Even Henry Sidney and Barnaby have learned to hold their tongues when it comes to the Duke of Northumberland. He dominates our king entirely, it seems."

"And through him, he dominates England!"

"Shh, Jane," Edward warned again. "No good

will come of speaking so. There's nothing to be done about it. Besides, the duke is only a duke. Once Edward is full grown he will have a mind of his own and the duke's influence will be less, I'm sure of it."

And if by any chance the king should be truly ill and not live to be full grown? Jane thought, not daring to speak the words out loud even to Edward. Why, then Princess Mary would be queen, and she would soon send the Duke of Northumberland packing.

And all the rest of us who have professed the new religion, Jane thought wryly. The thought of being sent packing away from court did not bother her overly much. In fact, the idea of living a peaceful life with Edward, far from the intrigues of court, tending to a houseful of children and with time to pursue her studies as much as she wished, was an idea which appealed to Jane greatly.

In any case, she told herself, the Duke of Northumberland is in no position to do harm to Edward or to myself. And the king is fifteen now. He will surely get well and will soon take matters into his own hands.

But the king did not get better. He grew steadily more and more ill until it was impossible to conceal it. In desperation, the Duke of Northumberland had him moved to the palace at Greenwich. It was hoped that the purer air there, away from the heat and stench of London, would help him to recover.

And, as the weeks went by, Jane's parents would still not discuss the subject of her marriage. They had an excuse now. "With the king so ill, Jane, how could you be so selfish as to think about your own affairs?" her mother expostulated when Jane finally dared to bring the subject up yet again.

"But, mother, I am past fifteen. This autumn I will be sixteen," Jane argued. "I am getting old!"

"Your father and I have your best interests at heart, child," the duchess replied. "You need not fear. We will see to it that you make the best match possible."

"But my marriage to Lord Edward *is* the best match possible. We are already betrothed —"

With an imperious wave of her hand, the duchess concluded the interview. "*We* will decide what is best for you, milady, and you will obey!"

With these ominous words, she swept out of the room, leaving Jane standing helplessly staring after her, and no amount of entreaty on Jane's part thereafter would make her say another word on the subject.

King Edward grew steadily worse. The Princess Mary had even come to London to see him, but it was three days before he could receive her. Edward told Jane privately that the only people allowed into the royal bedchamber now, besides his doctors and attendants, were the king's two closest friends, Henry Sidney and Barnaby Fitzpatrick — and, of course, the Duke of Northumberland.

"The duke is trying to persuade the king to sign something," Edward told Jane. "Henry caught him at it, although the duke concealed the parchment as soon as Henry entered the room. It looked like a devise of some kind. He was talking about the succession."

"The succession? To the throne? Why, the Princess Mary succeeds, of course. Who else?"

"Of course," Edward answered. "So it was decreed in King Henry's will. The Princess Mary and then the Princess Elizabeth. But there is something going on, Jane, and knowing the duke as I do, I am certain it is something wrong."

"I agree with you, Edward," Jane answered. "But what can he possibly do? There is no way he can benefit from our poor king's death. In fact, he is bound to suffer from it. The Princess Mary dislikes him as much as we do. She will have him away from court the minute she becomes queen, depend upon it."

"I know," Edward replied slowly. "But the wily duke knows that too. He is not the man to accept such a fate quietly. He is planning something, Jane. I would stake my life on it."

Unfortunately, Jane had to agree with Edward. And a cold fear took hold of her heart when her mother's words, "*We* will decide what is best for you, milady, and you will obey!" sprang into her mind, along with a picture of the Duke of Northumberland as he had looked the evening before. He had been to Sheen to dine with them and had spoken privately with her parents for a long time in the parlour afterwards. When he had emerged he was smiling — a greedy, triumphant smile. It was not the smile of a man who feared for his position. When he caught sight of Jane, his smile had widened and his eyes had gleamed with delight.

"And here she is herself!" he had cried. Almost as if, impossibly, she had been the subject of their conversation. He had thrown an arm around her shoulders in a familiar, almost fatherly way, not seeming to notice how she cringed away from him.

"Grown to be quite lovely, haven't you, my lady?" he had teased. There was a mocking, self-satisfied note in his voice that did not escape Jane. "And insistent upon being wed, your lady mother tells me," he went on. "How fortunate. How very fortunate indeed."

10
"Forgive me."

Two days later Jane found out exactly what the conspiracy between the Duke and Duchess of Suffolk and the Duke of Northumberland was. She was summoned abruptly into her parents' presence.

"We have made a decision regarding your future," the duchess announced. She was looking very smug and pleased with herself; the duke was actually beaming.

Jane stood as still as one of the great stones of Bradgate itself, hardly daring to breathe, let alone speak.

Her mother continued. "His grace, the Duke of Northumberland, has made a most fitting suggestion."

Jane stared at her, cold now in spite of the soft spring air that was wafting into the room.

"He has proposed a marriage between his youngest son, Guilford, and yourself. We agree that this would be a most suitable match, and we have accepted."

A vision of the pale, ingratiating young man she had seen at the birthday celebrations thrust itself into Jane's mind. Instantly she was as fiery hot as she had been cold before.

"I will not! Never!"

The broad, red face of the duchess purpled with fury. She lashed out at Jane, dealing her a blow with the back of her hand that sent the small figure sprawling in a heap on the floor.

Jane looked up, anger and hate blazing out of her eyes. "You may beat me until I am senseless, but I will not marry him!"

Her father was beside her in two quick strides. He raised his arm and hit her twice, once on either side of the head.

Jane felt her senses swimming.

"You will marry whomsoever your parents decree, milady," the duke roared. No one looking at him now would have recognized the handsome dandy of the court. Veins stood out starkly along his neck; his eyes were bulging from his head.

"I won't!"

The duke snatched up a riding whip and lashed Jane once, twice, then a third time across her face and shoulders.

Against her will, Jane cried out in pain. Tears sprang to her eyes. "But — Lord Edward!" she protested, forcing the words out. "I am betrothed to him."

"*Lord* indeed!" Her mother spat the words out venomously, her fury making her almost incoherent. "Your precious Edward is no longer Earl of Hertford, have you forgotten? He is no longer *Lord* anything."

"*We are betrothed!*"

"You are betrothed to Lord Guilford Dudley,

son of the Duke of Northumberland." Her father's hand was raised, poised ready to strike again. "You will consent to marry him, or I will beat you until you are dead!"

Jane stared up at the duke's raging face and knew that he meant it. Her ears were ringing with the violence of the blows she had received, her head reeling. She was very near fainting. Desperately she looked from him to her mother, then back again, then around her. They were alone. There was no help anywhere.

"I can't," she begged, her words barely audible. Then, involuntarily, she cringed as her mother moved towards her and towered over her threateningly.

The duchess looked as if her senses had taken leave of her entirely. Her face had darkened even more, and she was having trouble breathing.

"You ungrateful, trouble-making wretch of a girl! By God's bones — *I* will kill you!" Each word was forced out with an effort past her anger. Deliberately she raised her arm yet again and brought down her hand, fingers spiked with jewels, full across Jane's face.

Jane screamed once, then the pain and the blackness combined and she felt herself overwhelmed, racing, sinking, plunging into darkness.

* * *

For a week Jane was confined to her room with only Elizabeth Tylney and Mrs. Ellen to attend her. Once each day either her mother or her father, or both together, would visit her. They did not beat her again, perhaps because the bruises from their first beating were so frighteningly evident, but they threatened and cursed her continuously. The duchess, who appeared to be drinking even more heavily than usual, was particularly abusive. Jane stubbornly refused to consent to the marriage and begged to be allowed to send a note to Edward, but all to no avail. At the end of the week her parents suddenly stopped their visits. Jane was frantic to know what was going on.

"It's no use, my lady," Mrs. Ellen reported with a doleful face. "Plans for the wedding have already begun. It's to be held the end of next month. They mean to marry you whether or not you be willing, my lady."

"But they can't!" Jane protested. "I'm already betrothed. What do they say about that?"

"Nothing, my lady. It's as if the betrothal never existed. And poor Lord Edward has no one to speak for his rights now."

"I'll fight them," Jane vowed grimly. "Every step to the chapel and up to the priest. They'll have to drag me kicking and screaming."

"I fear, my lady, that if they have to, they will. They mean to see you married to Lord Guilford, and married you will be."

"But why? Why Guilford Dudley? His father's position is not that secure. If the king dies, God forbid, the Princess Mary will have him in the Tower and the old Duchess of Somerset released in a trice. Why, then, is the Duke of Northumberland's son so much more attractive to my parents than the son of the Duchess of Somerset?"

"The duchess *may* be released, and Lord Edward *may* regain his title and lands, but at the moment it is the Duke of Northumberland who holds power, my lady, and who sways the minds of their graces."

"And before him it was that infamous Thomas Seymour, the Lord High Admiral, and look what happened to him. It was only by sheer good fortune they weren't brought down with him. Will they never learn?"

Worse was to come. Early the next morning, Jane's sister Katherine burst into the room. Her face was red and swollen, and tears coursed down her cheeks.

"They mean to marry me off as well!" she burst out. "At the same time! When you marry Lord Guilford, I am to be wed to Lord Herbert! Jane, what can I do? He's detestable! I hate him! He sneers at me and only last month called me a little country bumpkin. Why are they doing this, Jane? What can we do?"

Jane stared at her sister, too shocked to answer. Katherine was still such a child. She was, if not exactly a "country bumpkin," an exceedingly young girl for her age and totally ignorant of the ways of the court. And Lord Herbert was definitely one of the least likable and most obnoxious of the young men at court. Why? Of course! His father, the Earl of Pembroke, was the closest confidant of the Duke of Northumberland. This was more of the duke's doing. He was tying Jane's family close to him and to his followers with ever-tightening bands. But why were they so important to him? *That* Jane still could not understand.

She reached out to comfort her sister, but her words were hollow. The trap, it seemed, had caught not only her but little Katherine as well.

* * *

A few days later a way out suddenly seemed to present itself. The king, surprisingly, requested Jane's presence at his bedside. The Duke of Northumberland had steadfastly refused to allow anyone to see the young king ever since he had been moved to Greenwich, but it seemed that he had rallied a little from his illness and was demanding to see Jane.

The Duke of Northumberland himself came to fetch her. He was obviously upset by the request, but not quite sure enough of himself yet to find a way of refusing to carry it out. His face was clouded and angry as he handed her none too gently into the barge that was to take them downriver.

Jane used the time they spent reaching Greenwich to compose in her mind what arguments she would use with the king in order to persuade him to intervene in the matter of her marriage and save her. Lord Edward was his close friend and cousin. The king loved him dearly and loved Jane as a sister. Surely he would help them. And if the king himself insisted that her betrothal to Edward be honoured, no one else could insist otherwise.

The Duke of Northumberland seemed to be

thinking along the same lines. He did not speak to Jane as they travelled, but his face grew darker and darker as they arrived and were led up the stairs towards the king's chamber. At the doorway he muffled an enraged oath when Henry Sidney stepped forward to bar his way.

"The king has requested that Lady Jane enter alone, your grace." The words were spoken respectfully, but hatred shone out of the young boy's eyes as he met the duke's angry stare.

For a moment it looked as if the duke might force himself in anyway. Then, to Jane's enormous relief, he stood back. Alone with Edward she had a chance!

But as soon as they entered the chamber, Henry caught Jane's arm and held her back. "My lady," he whispered, "wait."

Jane stopped. Indeed, for a moment she couldn't go on.

"His grace, the king, rallied for a while yesterday morn and was insistent upon seeing you. But now, I'm afraid —"

He did not need to continue.

All Jane's hopes had been smothered as soon as she had entered the chamber. The room was close and dark, lit only by a few candles. The window openings had been covered by heavy hangings and tapestries; a fire was raging in the fireplace. The heat was unbearable, but what was even worse was the stench.

Involuntarily, Jane put her hands up to cover her nose. What could cause such an odour? Then she looked towards the bed and realized, choking down rising nausea, that it was the king himself who was the source. With faltering steps she advanced, almost forgetting to make her obeisances. If she had, it was doubtful that the young king would have noticed.

He lay unmoving, only his head and one arm free of the mound of coverings upon him. Jane thought his eyes were closed, but it was hard to tell for certain, his face was so grotesquely swollen. His skin was distended and shiny, a yellow, waxy colour, his lips blue. The hand that rested on the counterpane was equally bloated. Only the puffy fingers, picking restlessly at the richly embroidered counterpane, gave any indication that he was alive.

Jane rose from her last curtsy and stood beside the bed, staring at the body of her cousin with horror. Here was no help for her. Here was death.

The king's eyes opened. He stared back up at Jane, the pupils dim and foggy. His mouth opened. For what seemed like an eternity, his lips struggled to frame a sound. Finally he succeeded.

"Jane." It was the barest of whispers.

"Oh, your grace! My cousin!" Jane threw herself onto her knees beside him. Forgetting all court procedure, she seized his hand in hers. It was burning hot, soft and almost obscenely yielding in her grasp.

Edward's eyes followed her with an effort. His mouth began its torturous workings again. Jane felt she couldn't bear it.

"Don't try to talk, cousin. Oh, dearest cousin, please don't try to talk. Rest."

Nevertheless, Edward's efforts continued.

138

There was something now in his eyes that Jane couldn't understand. Something that looked like pleading.

It must be fear, she thought. Fear — and pain.

"Be not frightened, cousin," she whispered. "God is with you. He will help you. He will comfort you."

Still Edward's lips moved, agonizingly. His eyes closed once again. He seemed exhausted by the effort, but just as Jane started to rise, he managed to speak. Two words. Two words that were inaudible to anyone in the room except Jane.

"What? Cousin, what do you mean?"

But his head had fallen to one side, and heavy, rasping, uneven breathing told Jane that the king was unconscious again.

She allowed herself to be helped up by Henry Sidney and led to the door. Once outside the room, she met the anxious eyes of the waiting Duke of Northumberland unseeingly.

What had her cousin meant? Two words only. Two words that had cost him such unbelievable effort: "Forgive me."

* * *

The weddings were to be held at Durham House, the London residence of the Duke of Northumberland. There were to be three weddings now, as the duke's daughter, also a Katherine, was to be married as well, to Lord Hastings, heir to the Earl of Huntingdon. The duke was building up his network with the craftiness of a spider, although try as she might, Jane could still not fathom his master plan. With the king obviously dying, he should be showing signs of worry. Instead he was ebullient. He showered Jane and her sister with gifts and, much to their mother's absolute delight, opened the wardrobes of the unfortunate Duchess of Somerset to her plunder. She availed herself of the most ornate and ostentatious robes, kirtles and fathingales, the most costly of the jewels, glorying in the booty. Jane watched with disgust as her mother gloated greedily over her spoils and bedecked herself outrageously. At the weddings, the duchess meant to cut the most dazzling figure the court had ever seen.

For her part, Jane was forced to submit to innumerable fittings of a costume which she had no intention of wearing. She was still determined not to go through with the ceremony, but bit by bit her endurance and resolve were being worn down. The Duke of Northumberland had sequestered Lord Edward. Jane had no idea where he was, and no one would tell her. Her parents made it abundantly clear that she would be constrained to carry through with the marriage, no matter what kind of resistance she put up. Still she fought. Then she found her sister Katherine, crumpled and crying in her room, bruised and shaken from a beating by her mother.

"They said I was encouraging you," Katherine sobbed. "They said that if I could not persuade you to consent to their wishes, they would beat me again."

Her parents had won. Jane finally gave in.

The day of the weddings dawned spitefully warm and sunny. The soft breezes of the beautiful late May day seemed to mock Jane as she was taken, mute and unresisting, to Durham House. Jane and Katherine, as well as the Duke of Northumberland's daughter, were shepherded into a large chamber upstairs to be robed and made ready for the weddings. Alone of the brides, the duke's daughter seemed untroubled. Jane looked wan and sick; little Katherine was terrified.

"Why do you not smile, my ladies?" Katherine Dudley asked. "Are you not as contented as I that your parents have found good husbands for you?"

"Are you so happy, then, with their choice?" Jane asked bitterly. "If so, you are much more fortunate than we."

"Happy? What does that have to do with it? I do my father's bidding. And so should you, my ladies." The duke's daughter's brow furrowed slightly with puzzlement. "After all," she continued, "we are only daughters, and the only good we can do in this world is through our marriages."

Jane turned away from her abruptly, fire raging through her at the servility of the other's acceptance. Then she sank back down into her own numbing despair. What was the difference? Whether they accepted it or not, the result was the same.

The triple wedding ceremony was to be one of the most costly and elaborate ceremonies that had taken place in London in years, apart from the king's coronation. All the nobles of the court and their ladies were present, all the most important personages of the day. King Edward was not able to be present, of course, but costly gifts of silver and gold plate had been sent in his name. The Princesses Mary and Elizabeth, however, had not been invited — the Duke of Northumberland had made certain of that. Not that Princess Mary would have come to such a strongly Protestant ceremony anyway, and Princess Elizabeth was still keeping very much to herself.

Durham House was transformed with bowers of flowers, brilliant banners, and hanging arras. The gardens through which the procession would pass had been trimmed and manicured and decorated with streamers and more banners. Jane herself was dressed in a shimmering gown of gold sewn with diamonds and pearls, with a mantle of silver tissue. Her hair was loose and hanging down her back, brushed to a burnished gold and plaited with flowers and strings of pearls. Before her was carried a golden bride cup hung with silken ribbons, with a branch of rosemary within. On either side of her walked a young boy with bride laces and rosemary tied to his sleeves. Behind her walked Katherine Dudley, then her own sister. Behind them followed a train of young girls, virgins all, some bearing bride cakes, others garlands ornamented with gold. Finally the bridegrooms walked in order, closely followed in turn by all the young men who were their friends.

Jane knew most of the young people who made up the procession, but she greeted no one.

There was only one way she would be able to get through this day. She deliberately let the numbness seep down through her and enfold her, shutting her off from all the rest of the world and blanketing her against the tumult around her. Her face stony, indifferent to the noise of the musicians that played all the way before her, she walked as one in a trance through the gardens, back to the house, and into the great hall where the ceremony was to be performed.

Her mind insensate, her eyes blank, she did not even hear the words as the Archbishop began a rolling, sonorous chant. It was not until she felt the shock of her hand being taken into someone else's that she abruptly came to an awareness of what was going on. Her vision cleared. She looked straight into the pale blue eyes of a youth who was awkwardly fitting a massive gold ring onto her finger.

He smiled once at her, complacently, then lifted his eyes with ostentatious devotion to the Archbishop.

Guilford Dudley. Her husband.

11
Queen Jane

Summer seemed to be exceedingly damp and rainy that year, Jane thought gloomily as she dragged herself out of bed, and that suited her mood exactly. She was hot and feverish again this morning; her head ached intolerably. Guilford had poked his head into her bedchamber earlier to enquire hopefully whether she would be up to riding with him later on. She had sent him off with a more than usually curt dismissal. The only good thing about this marriage, Jane reflected sourly, was the ease with which Guilford let himself be ordered around. Years of being his mother's youngest and favourite child had had their effect. He was as different from the rest of the hawkish Dudley brood as it was possible to be.

Jane called for Mrs. Ellen to help her. She had not been well ever since the wedding ceremony, but this morning she felt worse than usual.

"They are poisoning me," she muttered fretfully. "Now that they have claim to my family, they have no more use for me and they are poisoning me." She was only half serious, but Mrs. Ellen's eyes widened in horror.

"Oh, my lady! Say no such thing!"

"Did you send word to her grace that I would see her today?" Jane asked, ignoring her old nurse's outburst.

"Yes, my lady. She will send for you before dinner."

Jane splashed cool water on her flushed face. Surely this time the Duchess of Northumberland would allow her leave to return home for a visit. Jane had been begging for weeks now. She had been promised, after the marriage ceremony, that she could go back to her family, at least for a while, but permission had been steadfastly denied to her. The only measure of comfort she could take was in the knowledge that little Katherine had been allowed to go home with her mother right after the ceremony. Her marriage had not as yet been consummated, much to Jane's relief.

Unfortunately, she could not say the same for herself. Actually, Guilford had drunk so much and eaten so unwisely at the feast following the wedding that he had been ill for two days, but eventually he had recovered and had demanded that they begin living together as man and wife. It was her duty to obey, and she had, but her mouth twisted bitterly at the thought of his nightly visits. How different it would have been if it had been her beloved Edward. There would have been joy and love, instead of dread and passive submission. She shook her head, angry at her weakness. She had promised herself that she would not torment herself with impossible daydreams. Edward was lost to her forever. She was Lady Jane Dudley now — never again Lady Jane Grey. In spite of herself, her eyes filled with tears, and she splashed at her face again desperately.

Jane waited, but the duchess did not send for her before dinner. Indeed, the duchess was not even there for the noonday meal. She did not return to Durham Place until well on into the afternoon. By that time Jane was raging. She had worked herself into such a state that she was frantic. Her anger and her fever combined to the extent that she was almost incoherent when the summons to see her grace finally arrived.

Mrs. Ellen held Jane's arm and supported her as she made her way weakly to the duchess's apartments, clucking and worrying over her as if she were still a small child. Jane was too sick to object and, in fact, needed the support of the arm on which she leaned heavily. She staggered as she curtsied to the duchess, then regained her balance with difficulty.

The duchess's countenance was closed and cold as she looked at her daughter-in-law. "You wished to speak with me?"

"Your grace," Jane began weakly, then took a deep breath and forced herself to stand erect and meet the duchess's forbidding stare straight on. "Your grace," she repeated, more strongly, "I would beg leave to be allowed to return to my home to visit with my mother."

"Are you not content then, here with your

husband where you belong?" the duchess demanded, her brows lowering.

"I am not well, your grace. And it was promised to me before my wedding —" Jane faltered.

The duchess continued to stare at her for a long while before answering. Finally she broke her silence. "You look flushed. Are you really ill, then?"

"Yes, your grace. I fear it is a return of the fever from which I suffered before."

The duchess seemed to deliberate. Jane held her breath. She knew the woman's almost irrational fear of illness in those around her, and she was counting on this to secure her release, if only temporarily.

"Very well," the duchess said at last.

Jane sighed with relief and relaxed against the warm, soft bulk of Mrs. Ellen.

"But I will not have you at Suffolk Place," the duchess went on imperiously. "We are to Syon House this month. You will go to Chelsea Palace. Your lady mother may join you there, if she pleases. You have lived there before, you will be familiar enough with the surroundings — and you will be closer to us."

Chelsea Palace, where Jane had lived with Queen Katherine in happier times, was almost midway between London and the Dudley's residence of Syon House, farther upriver. Jane sighed again with relief. An escape, even only that far, seemed like an invitation to paradise right now.

* * *

Jane regained her health and her strength slowly

at Chelsea. The weather even co-operated, and the month of July began with bright, hot sunshine. Jane slowly relaxed, even began to smile again. She knew she was being held virtually a prisoner here at Chelsea — she was not allowed to leave the surrounding park, nor were any of her friends allowed to visit her — and she knew that eventually she would have to return to her husband, but for the time being she chose to put this knowledge out of her mind.

She sent for her books and began to study again. She missed her tutor. Perhaps, if she showed herself obedient enough, he might be allowed to return to her? Not very likely, she admitted sadly. She was a married woman now, with a married woman's responsibilities. No longer would she be given the time for unlimited, unaccountable study. Nevertheless, she took advantage of this interval and even regained a measure of her tranquillity.

At night, though, alone in her bed, she could not keep her mind busy as she did during the day, and her thoughts inevitably turned to Edward. Where was he? What was he doing? No one who knew would answer her questions. All Mrs. Ellen could find out was that he was still away from London.

Meanwhile the king's condition steadily grew worse. Rumours abounded now that he was dying. It was fast becoming impossible for the Privy Council to keep the truth from the people. Then, early one morning, Elizabeth Tylney stole into Jane's bedchamber.

"My lady," she whispered.

148

Jane roused herself sleepily and looked into the white, shocked face of her young lady-in-waiting. "What is it, Mistress Tylney?"

"They say the king is dead, my lady. There's whispers of naught else all around the town."

"But has an announcement been made?" Jane was wide awake instantly. Her poor cousin. She had not seen him again since her visit to him at Greenwich. She felt a wave of pity, mixed with relief that if this were true, his sufferings would finally be at an end. He would be with God, and all the useless, agonizing strife of this life would be finished. For a brief moment she felt almost envy.

Then another thought pushed in. If this were true, what would happen now? How quickly would the Princess Mary come to London and be proclaimed queen? And what would happen to the Dudleys — and to herself? The princess bore her no particular good will, Jane knew. For a moment she almost regretted her open criticism of Mary's religion; then she was immediately ashamed of herself. Did her own religion mean so little to her that she regretted defending it, for the sake of her own earthly comfort? She could not have done otherwise. But she was a Dudley now, and the fate of the Dudleys would be hers. No more daydreams of being sent away from court with Edward. Whatever fate the Princess Mary saw fit to award to the Duke of Northumberland, his daughter-in-law would share.

All that day the rumours flew. Work was left undone. Servants were scolded incessantly, but to no avail. Still there was no word. The next day was the same. More rumours abounded: the Princess Mary was on her way to London; the Princess Mary had fled to Spain; the king was recovering; the king was dead. The only sure fact in the world was that the Duke of Northumberland continued to wield authority and power and showed no signs of relinquishing it.

Then, on the evening of the third day, after Jane and her ladies had retired to her rooms, there was a sudden commotion at the water gate. Servants bustled out with torches; a hushed knot of cloaked figures was ushered into the palace. Jane's window overlooked the courtyard, but she could recognize no one in the dark. There was an urgent air of secrecy to the party, however. Before she could dispatch Mrs. Ellen to find out what was going on, a page appeared in Jane's doorway.

"An you please, my lady, there is a lady to see you."

Behind him stood a tall, cloaked figure.

Even as Jane signalled permission for her to come in, the woman moved forward. As she stepped into the flickering light of the fire, Jane recognized the Duke of Northumberland's daughter. Her face was strained and tense.

"You are to come with me, my lady. Immediately."

Jane stared at her, shocked by the abruptness of the command.

"We are to go to Syon House. You must make ready at once. My father has sent for you."

"At this hour? For what cause?"

"I know not, my lady. I was told only that it

was urgent, and I was to spare no time in getting you to Syon House. It is upriver, my lady, and the tide will be against us. Will you not come?"

Jane sensed that further questioning would be useless. The woman obviously knew no more than she. For a moment, however, she hesitated. Could this just be another trap? A way of getting her to return to her husband? No. There was no need for the duke to go to that much trouble. When he wanted her back he had only to tell her so and she would be forced to return. What then? What could possibly be the reason for this unseemly, mysterious summons?

The swift row up the river seemed to Jane to pass in a dream. Her confusion grew with each stroke of the oars. What puzzled her even more was the brief glimpse she had had of her mother as they left. The duchess had been standing in the doorway, staring after her with a look of fright, almost of terror on her face. What was happening?

They reached Syon House and made fast to the wharf. The water steps were slippery, and Jane stumbled as she climbed them. Hands reached out of the darkness to steady her. Footmen with torches came out to meet them and escort them across the gardens to the looming bulk of the house. In the house itself, at first, no lights were to be seen. Jane was led into the great hall, where only a few candles burned, and left there. The servants disappeared into the shadows. The hall was empty and echoing. Tapestries — spoils from innumerable Catholic churches — hung ghost-like in the gloom. Jane tensed herself and stood, alone, almost paralyzed with an ominous forboding.

Suddenly the darkness was lightened by the flickering of more candles, and hard footsteps sounded. The Duke of Northumberland strode into the room, closely followed by the Earls of Huntingdon and Pembroke. To Jane's confusion and consternation, the three lords knelt in front of her. Then, even as she protested, the Duke of Northumberland kissed her hand and rose quickly to his feet.

"Follow me, your grace," he said. In spite of his outward show of obeisance, it was an order. Before Jane could question him, or try to make any sense out of the proceedings, he turned and led the way out of the room. She was forced to follow him.

With the two earls close behind, they climbed the stairs and made their way into the long gallery. To Jane's further astonishment, the duke led her up onto the dais under the canopy reserved for royal personages. As she followed him, almost skipping in her effort to keep up with his long strides, she realized that all the other lords of the Privy Council were assembled in the room. Even her father was there! And Guilford! As soon as they saw her, with one accord, they all sank to their knees.

Jane stared at their lowered heads, her mind leaping away from the impossibility of what was happening. "My lords —" she began.

"Your grace," the duke forestalled her, his black eyes meeting hers with a tense, triumphant, unyielding blaze. "The king is dead. He has named you, your grace, as his heir." He turned to the kneeling peers and swept them to their feet with an imperious wave of his hand.

"Long live Queen Jane!" he cried.

Their voices echoed his.

"But the Princess Mary! King Henry's will!" Jane's voice was shaking uncontrollably.

"It is King *Edward's* devise that will have its way, your grace, and he has, in his wisdom, decreed that you shall succeed him." The words poured out smoothly, as if oiled and well rehearsed, but there was a thread of steel running through them.

Jane shook her head, still uncomprehending. "But how? For what reason has the Princess Mary been disallowed? And the Princess Elizabeth?" she added. Both princesses had been named in King Henry's will.

"Bastards both, your grace. Named so by King Henry himself. And should we entrust the kingdom to one who would bring back the idolatry of popishness? England needs a Protestant queen and a true-born queen, not a papist nor the dubious daughter of a whore!"

Into Jane's mind flashed the memory of Edward's coronation. The Archbishop's words suddenly sounded as clearly as if they were being spoken in the room at that very moment: "Sirs, here present is Edward, rightful and undoubted inheritor by the laws of God and man to the Crown . . ."

Rightful and undoubted inheritor by the laws of God and man to the Crown.

"The crown is not my right!" Jane cried,

153

breaking into tears as she felt the hollow surge of panic overwhelm her. "I cannot accept! The Princess Mary is the rightful heir. In the sight of England — in the sight of God!"

Her father was at her side immediately. "It is too late, daughter. The thing is done. At this very moment the proclamations are being read out on all the street corners of London and at all the crossroads. *Jane* is Queen of England."

"Not if I do not accept! You cannot force me to this, father, as you forced me to marriage!"

"And would you, then, have my death on your conscience? And the deaths of your husband and father-in-law? We have all assisted in this undertaking, have sworn allegiance to you as our queen. If you refuse and Mary becomes queen, the heads of every one of us will be forfeit. Will you have that on your conscience, daughter?"

Jane wavered as the full enormity of the situation overpowered her. Then, suddenly, another thought occurred to her. "My mother," she barely whispered, searching desperately for a way out. "Surely if the princesses be truly disallowed, then the crown should fall to her before me?"

"Your mother has graciously given way to you, my lady," the Duke of Northumberland put in quickly. "She sees the wisdom and necessity of England's having a young and healthy queen to govern her for years to come. And to establish a dynasty — a line of heirs that cannot be contested."

Guilford also stepped forward and knelt before her again, grasping her hand in his. "My lady, you *must* consent! As your lord husband I could command you, but instead I entreat you. We have all enmeshed ourselves in this matter too thoroughly to escape it now. Your lord father is right — it is too late. You *must* consent. Would you have the deaths of us all to your account?" His voice wavered at this last, and his mouth trembled. Clearly he was terrified at the thought of her refusing.

Jane looked at him helplessly. Then she looked around at the faces surrounding her — the duke's, hard and uncompromising; her father's, pleading. Her father, too, seemed frightened, as if he had only just now realized the enormity of what they had done. Jane sank to her knees and buried her face in her hands.

"Guide me, oh God," she prayed. "Help me! Show me the way. Show me Thy will . . ."

They were right. Her father, the Duke of Northumberland, Guilford — they would all be condemned to death if she refused the crown. They had gone too far. It *was* too late. There was no love in her heart for any of them, but could she bring herself to be responsible for their deaths? Where did her duty lie? Was it God's will that she should be queen? If it were, she would accept the burden, however frightened she might be of it. But was it truly God's will? Did He direct Edward to change the succession, or was this somehow just another one of the wily Duke of Northumberland's plots? But if she refused . . . Could God really mean her to be responsible for the deaths of so many?

Her head whirled, and even as she knelt, she could feel the old familiar fever reaching for her again. Her cheeks began to flush and burn, her mind to reel under the confusion.

"Rise, your grace. I will escort you to your chambers."

The voice of the Duke of Northumberland was uncharacteristically soft, almost sympathetic. It caught her off guard. Unwittingly, Jane responded to it. She allowed him to help her to her feet.

The assembled lords fell to their knees before her once more, heads bowed. Their shadows danced and flickered like insane devils in the uncertain, wavering light of the candlelit chamber.

Before Jane could collect herself, before she could even utter another word, the duke led her past them and out of the room.

12
The trap behind the crown

There was no sleep for Jane that night. She remained on her knees all through the dark hours, praying for guidance and strength from God. Morning found her wan and exhausted, still feverish and confused. But there was to be no rest for her then either. The sun had barely risen when she was summoned out of her bedchamber. Holding tightly onto her old nurse's arm, she emerged to find the Duke of Northumberland waiting. His piercing black eyes swept over her, then he sank into an exaggerated obeisance.

"Your grace!"

"I have not — I am still not certain —" Jane's voice was so weak as to be barely audible.

The duke rose swiftly. "Your grace, it is God's will! Would you deny the will of God as evidenced through the hand of your own dearly beloved cousin, God rest his soul?"

Jane stared at him mutely.

"In any case, your grace, the deed is done," he repeated. "Since last even the name of Queen Jane has been proclaimed throughout the land.

The people are gathering to greet you, the royal procession to the Tower has been planned. There is already celebration and joy throughout the city." He paused. "You *are* the queen!" There was a note of steel in his voice. His eyes bored into Jane's until she felt that it was only the force of his will that was keeping her on her feet.

"Dear God," she murmured, "if it be Thy will —"

"It is!"

Jane closed her eyes, breaking the contact, and slumped against Mrs. Ellen.

"Very well," she whispered. "So be it." Instantly she was in a panic, but before she could recover herself, as if on cue, her mother swept into the room followed by a whole retinue of seamstresses and fitters.

Immediately Jane became the centre of a mad hubbub of activity, alternately curtsied to and pulled this way and that as she was readied for her presentation to the populace of London. The poor Duchess of Somerset's wardrobe was being raided yet again. Jane felt she would sink under the weight of the robes and jewels that were being pressed upon her.

Syon House was soon completely enveloped in turmoil. In addition to the seamstresses and fitters, the house and courtyards were filled to overflowing with footmen, bargemen, and halberdiers, all milling around, receiving orders and shouting commands in their turn. But in the midst of all the hysteria, all the noise and pandemonium, one thought only was uppermost in

Jane's mind: she had acquiesced. She was queen of England.

*   *   *

By three o'clock in the afternoon, the procession of barges that would take them to the Tower of London was ready. Jane, as was the custom of the kings and queens of England, would remain in the Tower with her family and the lords of the Privy Council until her coronation.

At last, Jane stepped forth into the waiting horde of nobles and courtiers attired as a queen. She wore a richly brocaded kirtle and long-sleeved bodice of Tudor colours — white and green — all lavishly embroidered with gold. On the shining cap of her hair was placed a white coif set with diamonds, rubies, and pearls. Guilford was waiting to take her hand. He also was attired in splendid doublet and hose of white and gold satin, which set off his height and fairness to perfection. Together they made a picture of dazzling beauty.

Guilford was beaming happily and obviously delighted with the proceedings, his fears put to rest. Outwardly stony cold now, Jane walked with him between the double row of magnificently dressed people who swept into deep obeisances as she passed by. Inwardly, though, she was still being torn apart by a raging tumult of feelings such as she had never before known.

As they continued, a major flaw in all the careful planning became apparent. Jane was so tiny, walking alongside her tall husband, that no one except those in the very front of the crowd could see even the top of her head. A flurry of dismay ensued — the waiting populace must be able to see its new queen — then the solution was quickly found. From somewhere, someone produced a pair of wooden chopines, fully three inches high, which were strapped onto her feet. That solved the problem for the crowds who wished to see their new queen, but posed another one for the queen herself. She was now forced to clutch onto Guilford for support and totter precariously down to the waiting barge.

By four o'clock the tide was full out and the procession was on its way. There had been storms in the air after the king's death, but this day the weather was still and bright. The sunlight was caught, reflected, and thrown back thousands of times off the jewelled finery, sword hilts, and gaily plumed hats that bedecked the occupants of the state barges. Gold and silver tissues, multi-coloured damasks and satins, the busy, keyed-up chattering of everyone but Jane — all combined to provide a welter of colour and excitement.

Jane stared past the excitement of those around her and silently scanned the shores. She had never felt sick in a boat before, but today it was taking all of her will to master the nausea that threatened to overpower her. At first there were few people to be seen, then, as they swept into London, growing crowds lined the banks. But where was the celebration, the joy that the duke had spoken of so confidently?

The Tower loomed into view and the cannon thundered a salute. The noise was deafening, but from the rows and rows of people on the banks there came not a sound. They had wakened that morning to find that their king was dead and to listen to the proclamation of an unwanted, unknown cousin as queen of England. Who amongst them had ever heard of Lady Jane Dudley? All they knew was that she was the daughter-in-law of the Duke of Northumberland — the most hated and feared man in England by now. Anger and resentment met Jane's gaze on all sides as they watched this puppet girl who had been set above the Princess Mary. The knots of archers who had been hired to shout and fling their caps in the air as the heralds blew their trumpets and proclaimed the new queen only served to emphasize the silence of the rest.

Jane looked, and recognized the resentment. "They do not want me," she whispered, but her words went unheard in the general hilarity on board her barge. She looked again, and remembered the cheering and wild celebration of Edward's procession to Westminster Palace. A coldness which had nothing whatsoever to do with the wind pervaded her body.

They reached the water gate of the Tower and prepared to disembark. Jane was handed a posy of blossoms and herbs to hold to her nose as she was assisted over the bridge across the foul-smelling moat, but not even these spicy, pungent aromas could mask the choking stench of the foul water beneath them. All the sewers of London drained into this moat. She buried her nose in the small bouquet and hastened across and through the Queen's Gate.

On the other side waited the nobles and most

161

high personages in all England. Here was no silence and resentment, but celebration and pomp and ceremony enough to welcome the most joyful of princes. It should have drowned out any qualms, but it didn't. The memory of the silent, staring faces of the ordinary folk stood squarely between her and the richly-dressed, fawning personages in front of her. Jane drew a deep breath and tightened all her being into a hard, resilient shell. This must be borne. She must get through it.

On the threshold of the Tower grounds waited the Marquis of Winchester, the Lord Treasurer, and Sir John Bridges, the Lieutenant of the Tower. They were surrounded by civilian and military officials and backed by the Yeomen of the Guard, each with his gilded axe over his shoulder. The Archbishop of Canterbury stood waiting to bless the new queen. Beyond him waited the Duke and Duchess of Northumberland and Jane's parents, the Duke and Duchess of Suffolk.

Winchester knelt to deliver the keys to the fortress. The Duke of Northumberland stepped forward quickly, took them, and handed them to Jane. Jane received them, then the procession formed again and moved forward to the sound of guns crackling and roaring. Jane's mother, herself, carried her daughter's train.

Smoke enveloped the turrets, veiling gilded cupolas and silken flags momentarily, then wisping away to leave the flags tossing in the breeze. Ravens croaked and fluttered out of the way as the procession moved past. Bowing courtiers and statesmen, kneeling pages, curtseying ladies lined the slope leading up to the White Tower and the Royal Apartments. Past them was the dark, squat chapel of St. Peter ad Vincula — the sad last resting place of Henry's two doomed wives, Anne Boleyn and Catherine Howard. Jane looked at the chapel, then turned her eyes away. Those had been unfortunate queens. Would she be destined to join them?

She squared her small shoulders and lifted her head high. If she were trembling, no one should see it. Whatever the outcome, the course was set and she must follow it. Cheers rang out; petals rained down and covered her path. Unseeing, her eyes lifted to the blue, vaulted sky above, Jane silently committed herself to God's will and walked steadily on, her tiny, chopine-laden feet setting themselves down purposefully, one after the other, carrying her onto and across the waiting, sunny square of Tower Green.

*   *   *

Jane was led into the White Tower, then on down to the Presence Chamber where she took her place under the state canopy. Winchester, the Lord Treasurer, left but returned almost immediately. Behind him trailed a procession of pages carrying various coffers and boxes. To Jane's dismay, however, the Lord Treasurer himself was carrying the Crown Imperial of the realm!

"Your majesty," he began, holding the crown out towards her, "will you most graciously consent to accept this?"

163

Jane shrank back from the jewelled purple velvet cap as if it were capable of destroying her.

"My lord!" she gasped. "Only when I have been crowned in the presence of God and His witnesses, by His own representative here on earth, may I wear the crown. It is blasphemy to handle it in this manner!"

"But, your grace," Lord Winchester persisted, smiling encouragingly, "we mean just to try it on. To see if it fits, your grace."

"Yes, your majesty," the Duke of Northumberland added ingratiatingly. "Try. We shall see how it becomes you."

"No, my lords," Jane begged. "I cannot do such a thing! It is against God's laws. Only from the Archbishop himself may I accept such a holy burden." She was almost in tears.

"Your grace, try," the Duke of Northumberland insisted. "We must know before the coronation whether it should be altered. It is the custom. And after we have fitted it properly to you, then we shall begin forthwith with the making of another to crown your husband."

With these words, in spite of her confusion and fear, Jane suddenly saw the whole pattern of the treachery of the duke's actions. He had been planning this for months, ever since he had known that the king would probably die! That was why he had insisted on her marriage to Guilford. He had contrived to make the king change his father's will — that was the parchment Henry Sidney had spoken of — and then he had struck a bargain with her parents. The Duchess of Suffolk would renounce her claim to the throne, and in return he would make Jane queen of England.

And Jane would make his son, Guilford, king. That was his ultimate plan. And once Guilford was king . . . Jane did not need to puzzle long about that. A king took precedence over his queen, no matter who was the rightful inheritor to the throne. Once Guilford was king, England would be under his rule, not hers. *And* under the rule of the Duke of Northumberland himself. It had been a trap, and she was caught in it inextricably. The cold knowledge settled over her like a shroud. But at the same time, it blanketed the fever, quelled the nausea, dispelled the confusion.

"Never!"

Small, terrified, but furious now, Jane drew herself up to her full height and glared back at the startled duke. "You have forced me to be queen — and by God's mercy I pray we do not all regret it — but I will not name Guilford king. Never! He may be a duke, but never king over me!"

"Your grace! He is your husband!" The Duchess of Northumberland was the first to react.

Guilford himself was close behind. "My lady, why should you hesitate? Surely it is mete that I, your lawful husband, be made king? How unseemly it would be if England were to be ruled by a queen with but a *duke* for a husband."

"I pray you, your grace, reconsider." The Duke of Northumberland had recovered his composure, and the tone of his voice was threatening but confident. "It is your duty."

"My lady wife, I beseech you!" Guilford imp-
lored again. "I never dreamt you would refuse!"

Jane looked around her. Even her parents
seemed aghast. Guilford was so distressed he was
wringing his hands and — surely that was not a
gleam of tears in his eyes! She looked at him with
pity mingled with contempt. So they had all been
in on it. Unbeknownst to her, this is what they
had been planning all along. Well, they had
finally outwitted themselves. They had made her
queen — queen she would be! She turned to face
the Duke of Northumberland defiantly.

"My *duty* is to uphold Parliament and do
nothing of this sort without their consent. It
would be unlawful. It is within my power to
create my husband duke, no more. Anything further must be accomplished by an act of Parliament." And never will be as long as I am queen,
she added silently to herself. "Surely your grace
knows the laws of England as well as I?" The last
was a deliberate taunt, as insulting as Jane could
make it.

The Duke of Northumberland flushed, but
was prevented from saying anything more by
Lord Winchester, who motioned forward the
pages bearing the coffers and boxes he had
brought with him.

"Your grace," he interjected quickly in a con-
ciliatory tone. "You will, in any case, accept
these, the Crown Jewels, I pray. They are yours
now, to be left in your safekeeping." As he spoke,
the pages deposited their burdens on the carpet
at her feet. There was nothing Jane could do in
this instance but accept.

Mercifully, the Lord Treasurer then begged leave to quit her presence and backed out, bowing, taking the Crown Imperial with him. That battle, at least, Jane had won.

Guilford began to speak again, but a wave of the hand from his father silenced him quickly. The duke knew that Jane was right. "We shall speak of this matter later," he said stiffly.

Jane had won that battle as well, at least temporarily, but a glance at the Duchess of Northumberland's face, suffused with anger, and at Guilford's sulky countenance, told her that she had won at a cost. And the duke would not give in so quickly — there was no hope of that. He would never allow all his plans to be dashed so easily. The look on his face as he glared at Jane was murderous.

"My son and I will leave, then, with your grace's permission," the duchess announced with barely concealed contempt.

"Nay, madam," Jane replied quickly. "Even as you insisted that I remain at my husband's side when we were married, now I must insist that my husband remain at my side until my coronation. The people of England, it would seem, are suspicious of me already — it would not do to set tongues a-wagging further by a husband who will not consort with his wife. Lord Guilford must remain here."

There was a moment's incredulous silence as the duchess glowered at Jane. Jane, however, held her ground. Finally the duchess lowered her eyes and swept into a low curtsy. "As you will, your grace," she muttered through clenched teeth. "Lord Guilford will stay."

13

A time to be born . . .

Two days later Jane was almost beginning to regret her decision. Guilford sulked and whined constantly, and complained that not nearly enough attention was being paid to him. The Duchess of Northumberland — who had elected to stay with her son — and the Duchess of Suffolk wrangled and fought incessantly over the matter of whether he should or should not be made king. Jane was ill again with her old fever and an intolerably aching head. In desperation, she ordered that Guilford was to be served on the knee and addressed as "your grace," the outward signs of kingship. He was allowed to sit under the canopy of state beside her at her own level, as well, but even that did not satisfy him. Further than that, however, Jane would not go.

The days had been full. The Privy Council met each morning and afternoon. Ill or not, Jane was determined to take her part in the proceedings and insisted on being given a report at the end of each meeting. There were announcements to be sent out to the representatives of France and Spain declaring her accession to the throne, papers to be signed. The date of the coronation had been set for a fortnight later, and preparations for this all-important event were underway. Under all, however, there persisted a deep sense of uneasiness. Nowhere in London was there any sign of rejoicing or celebration. The people went about their business silently, sullenly. And there was an ominous silence from the Lady Mary, as she was now being called. The Duke of Northumberland had sent her an announcement of Jane's accession as soon as the deed had been accomplished, but there had as yet been no reply.

Then, on the evening of the eleventh of July, while Jane, her family, and the members of the Council were at supper, a messenger arrived. He insisted that his message was for the Duke of Northumberland only, and that it was urgent. Exhausted and mud-spattered as he was, he was ushered into the assembled gathering.

"Your grace," he panted, bowing low before Jane. Then he handed his parchment to the Duke of Northumberland.

There was complete silence as the duke read it. His face was impassive, giving nothing away. Finally he looked up. "Your errand has been completed," he said shortly to the waiting messenger. "Leave us."

When the boy had gone, the duke, ignoring Jane completely, turned to the other members of the Council. "The Lady Mary asserts her right to the throne. She is marching on London with a goodly troop to claim it."

The Duchess of Suffolk immediately broke into a wail.

170

The Duchess of Northumberland echoed her. "My lord, what is to be done? We are lost!"

"Hush your wailings!" The duke was too upset to even to try to observe the usual courtesies. "Send my sons Warwick and Robert to me. They shall raise an army to quash this uprising before it is fairly begun!"

Jane watched in horror as the preparations for battle were hastily organized. There would be bloodshed! For her right to the throne! In vain she pleaded with the duke to abstain.

"This is wrong, my lord!" she cried. "We *cannot* carry on with this! Send word to the Princess Mary that I give in to her freely, that I acknowledge her right before mine. I beg of you, my lord!"

"You are a foolish child," the duke retorted. "Do you think she will pardon us for this? If the Lady Mary takes the crown, we will all die — you first of all, my lady. What we have committed is high treason, have no doubt of it, and you are as guilty as any of us!"

"Then I'll die! If it be God's will, if I have sinned in allowing this crown to be thrust upon me, then I will die!"

"Well, *I* won't. We *will* do battle, your grace. And we *will* win!" The duke strode angrily from Jane's presence.

His sons met, however, not the small force they had expected, but a strong and defiant princess at the head of a large and ever-growing horde. The people of England were flocking to her from all sides. The duke's sons were completely routed and barely escaped with their lives. Mary was now in command of an army more than five thousand strong.

In desperation, the Duke of Northumberland took over the leadership of Queen Jane's army and rode forth to meet the Lady Mary. He had wanted to send the Duke of Suffolk in his stead, not trusting the loyalty of the lords he would leave behind, but Jane would not allow that. Frightened as she was of her father at times, she was even more terrified of being left alone in the duke's power. He had more than amply demonstrated that he expected his wishes to be obeyed, not hers, but in this instance Jane had her way.

Soon after he left, however, reports began to flood back that the people would not rally to him as they might have done to the Duke of Suffolk. The Duke of Northumberland had made too many enemies; he was hated and despised in too many quarters. The lords of the Privy Council, too, began murmuring uneasily. The duke had been well-advised to distrust them — they hated him as much as did the rest of England. Rumours now came back that the duke's own army was deserting to the other side. Twice he requested reinforcements, twice the lords demurred.

Then news was brought that Mary had been proclaimed queen in Oxford. That night both the Lords Pembroke and Winchester left the Tower without advising Jane and returned to their houses. It smelled like desertion, and Jane reacted quickly, sending soldiers to have them fetched back. When they returned, in desperation she gave orders that all the gates were to be locked and the keys brought to her by seven o'clock every night. She had not yet been queen for a week, but already deceit and treachery hung in the very air around her. If she wanted to survive, she must recognize and conquer it.

Northumberland was forced to retreat towards London. The guards around the Tower were doubled. The lords of the Privy Council, including Pembroke and Winchester, requested an audience with the queen.

Jane received them.

"Your grace," Lord Pembroke said, kneeling at her feet, "the battle does not go well. We beg permission of your majesty to allow us to leave the Tower and negotiate with the envoy from France. He will give us aid. Only thus can we survive the onslaught."

His manner was obedient and reverential, but Jane believed none of his words. It was a trick, she was certain of it. But what was she to do? The decision to make battle in the first place had been taken out of her hands — events were completely out of her control. Where did her duty lie now? There was nothing more she could do. Nothing except put her trust in God and submit herself to His will. She hesitated, then turned away. "Go, then," she said in a voice so low they strained to hear it. "Do what you must."

The next day word was sent to the Tower that the lords of the Privy Council had declared for the Princess Mary. They had demanded the return and the surrender of Northumberland, then had trooped off to celebrate Catholic Mass in the Cathedral of St. Paul's. The Duke of Suffolk himself brought the news to his daughter. With his own hands he tore down the state canopy under which she sat.

"These things are not for you now, my daughter," he said. His voice trembled and his eyes, usually so proud and haughty, were filled with tears.

"Nor did I ever want them," Jane replied. A deep sense of relief flowed through every part of her. It was over. For the first time in nine days she felt at peace. "Out of obedience to you and my mother I have grievously sinned." She paused. "What do we do now, father?"

The duke avoided her eyes. "I do not know," he said, controlling himself with an effort. "We must wait here upon the decision of the Council."

Jane nodded.

But when supper was served that evening, the Duke and Duchess of Suffolk were not there. They and the Duchess of Northumberland had fled the Tower, throwing themselves on the mercy of the Council and loudly proclaiming Mary as queen. Guilford and Jane were left alone.

*   *   *

They were moved out of the Royal Apartments of the White Tower the next day. Guilford was removed to the Beauchamp Tower, where he was kept in close confinement in a small, semi-circular room at the very top. Jane was taken to the Gentleman-Gaoler's lodging, which was one of the little houses that lined Tower Green. Mrs. Ellen and Elizabeth Tylney were allowed to remain with her; she was also permitted to keep one page.

The Gentleman-Gaoler, Mr. Partridge, and his wife were good-hearted, simple people who, once they got over their initial awe at being the gaolers of such an important personage, were anxious to help Jane in any way they could. They made her and her ladies as comfortable as possible in two upstairs rooms.

The morning after their move, Lord Winchester came to reclaim the Crown Jewels. He went first to the White Tower, then to the house where Jane was being kept prisoner.

"My lady," he said brusquely, "there is a discrepancy. Some of the belongings of the former queens are missing from the coffers." His manner was far different from the fawning obsequiousness with which he had greeted Jane upon her arrival to the Tower as queen.

Jane stared back at him with as much haughtiness as she could muster. There had been all manner of trinkets and trifles in the coffers as well as the Crown Jewels — gold buttons, pins, brooches, tiny enamelled boxes, and jewelled clocks. Jane had not had time nor inclination to look at half of them.

"I have no knowledge of anything missing, my lord," she replied. "They are all as I left them, as you brought them."

"Nevertheless, items are missing, my lady. Until such time as they can be located, I will have to ask you to make restitution."

"Make restitution? With what? With the few poor coins I have now in my possession?"

"Yes, my lady. And with any other jewels or valuables that you might have here with you."

Trembling with anger, Jane dispatched Mrs. Ellen to collect what little she had. As she handed them over to the Lord Treasurer, her lips curled with contempt. "To what poor duties you have been brought, my lord," she said. "It would seem you have fallen lower than I if you must needs resort to robbing a woman from whom all else has been taken."

Lord Winchester flushed. Without replying, he sketched a hurried bow and left.

"They have done the same to Lord Guilford," Mrs. Ellen reported indignantly later on that same day. "Taken all he had!"

"It would seem they will not run the risk of us bribing any gaolers for our release," Jane replied. "We must be very precious indeed, if they go to such lengths to ensure we cannot escape."

On the third day of August, Mary finally arrived, triumphant, in London. Jane was awakened by the sound of guns and cannons firing in welcome. She dashed to her small back window, but could see little beyond the Tower walls. The noise of cheering and celebration came clearly up to her, however. Here, finally, was the rejoicing and welcome for their new queen — Henry's own daughter — which had been so conspicuously missing from Jane's procession.

"Excuse me, my lady, but I have received orders that you are to stay within today." Mrs. Partidge stopped Jane with considerable embarrassment as she was about to leave the house for her customary early morning walk around the

176

Green. "They say the queen will be coming to release the old prisoners as soon as possible."

In the late afternoon Mary did, indeed, enter the Tower at the head of her triumphant procession. Jane, standing at the tiny window which overlooked the Green, could see it all.

The queen, riding a scarlet-caparisoned, sedate mare, looked pleased with her reception within the Tower, but much older than Jane remembered. Her sallow, dark face was pinched and drawn. There had been many reports of ill health during the past years, and it looked as if they were well founded.

The figure to whom Jane's eyes were immediately drawn, however, rode directly behind the queen. It was the Princess Elizabeth, drawn out of her self-imposed, protective isolation at last. Her flaming red hair flowed over her shoulders and back in a cascade of undisciplined curls. She sat her prancing white mare with ease and confidence, smiling radiantly at the assembled throng. It was she, rather than her sister, Jane thought, who looked every inch the queen.

"Who is to be released?" Jane asked Mrs. Ellen, who had come to stand beside her.

"The Duchess of Somerset, my lady. And poor Lord Courtenay, who has been imprisoned since the reign of old King Henry."

"What of my father? And the Duke of Northumberland?"

Both the Duke of Suffolk — his declaration for Mary notwithstanding — and the Duke of Northumberland had been imprisoned soon after

Jane and Guilford's arrest. Guilford's brothers, also, had joined him in Beauchamp Tower.

"Your lord father has been pardoned, my lady, and your lady mother received back with all love and friendliness by her grace, Queen Mary, but the Duke of Northumberland's trial has been set and they say there is no way he will avoid the executioner's block."

"It is very hard to find any pity in my heart for the duke," Jane replied quietly. "Still, we are taught that we must forgive our enemies. What amazes me most is that my lord father has once again wriggled away from the results of his conniving. I confess, I do not see how he can do it. I suppose I should rejoice for him and my lady mother." She sighed. She was obviously not to be included in her parents' pardon. She wondered if they had even asked the queen on her behalf.

The next evening Jane set herself to writing a letter to Queen Mary. She knew she must admit that she had sinned in accepting the crown; she must beg Mary's mercy, trusting the queen would realize that the plot was not of her doing, but had been forced upon her. It was a difficult letter to write. One part of her acknowledged that it was something that should be done, something she owed in duty to her queen; another part stubbornly insisted that it was not her sin at all, but the sin of those around her. It wounded her dignity to beg for mercy. Still, for Guilford's sake if not for her own, she must do it. She had not seen him since their imprisonment, but Mrs. Ellen had told her that he was taking his fate very badly and was suffering.

"He spends most of his days in tears, my lady, carving your name over and over in the stone of his prison walls." Mrs. Ellen was obviously scornful, but Jane felt only compassion for him now. He was not as strong as she, but his weakness was not of his own doing.

As she laboured over her letter, straining to see by the stub of a single candle guttering in the fast fading light, there was a tap at her door.

"There is someone to see you, my lady," her page announced.

Jane straightened up and rubbed at her tired eyes. Who could be calling on her here? She was not allowed to see anyone — there was no one she knew who wished to see her now anyway.

As she descended the narrow wooden stairs, she looked with puzzlement at the tall figure who stood with his back towards her, just inside the door. There was something familiar about him. Then he turned, and she clutched at the handrail for support.

It was Edward.

"Jane —" Edward breathed her name, but made no move towards her.

Jane, for her part, felt that if she loosened her hold on the handrail she would surely fall to the floor in a heap. She couldn't even speak.

"You look pale. Are you ill?"

"I have been. I'm well now." For a moment Jane wondered if she were imagining the whole scene. If, in reality, she were not well yet and all this was nothing but an hallucination. "Edward, are you really here?"

"I am, my lady."

"But — but how?"

"The queen" — he stumbled over the words, then went on quickly — "the queen has restored our lands to us. I think she will even restore my title. She has been most gracious to my lady mother and myself."

"She allowed you to come here?"

"No. This was done by stealth and must not be repeated, for your sake especially. Queen Mary is inclined to pity you and be merciful towards you — we must not risk doing anything that would change that. But I had to come just once. See you just once more, though I know you are lost to me forever." His voice broke.

"Oh, Edward. How I wish that matters had not turned out this way. How I wish —"

Finally Edward moved. He stepped forward and reached out to place his hand over hers on the handrail. "And I, my beloved."

For a long moment neither spoke. Then Jane seemed to gather her strength. "Can you come and sit for a while with me, or must you return immediately?"

"I cannot stay. I cannot risk being discovered here."

"You can never stay. We have never had enough time . . ." Jane's voice trailed off. Then she collected herself again. "Before you go, then, there is one thing I must beg of you."

"I will do anything that is within my power for you, you must know that."

"It is for my sister Katherine. I am worried for her. I do not know what has happened to her."

"Then rest your mind, my lady. I can reassure you on that matter this minute. Her marriage to Pembroke's rascally son has been dissolved, and she is still safe at Suffolk Place with your mother."

Jane sighed with relief. She had been so afraid that somehow Katherine would also suffer for her mistakes. "She is so young, Edward. And so unwise in the ways of the world. I fear for her. I fear that my parents might stake their thwarted ambitions on her now. Will you take care of her for me, Edward? As much as you can? Be her friend?"

"I will, my lady, I vow it. But trust in God's mercy and mayhap you will be there to take care of her yourself ere long. The queen fears you not, and if there is no undue protest from the Protestants about the restoration of her own religion, I'm certain she will set you free."

"Do you really believe that, Edward? Is it possible?"

"Yes. I believe it with all my heart. The duke was the instigator of this treason — he will be punished. You and your unfortunate husband were but innocent pawns. Her grace bears you no malice. There will be a trial — there must be that — but surely you will be pardoned and set free."

Suddenly the rest of Edward's words sank in. "You said 'the restoration of her own religion.' So England is once again papist?"

"Yes, I fear so. But there is no persecution of the Protestants. The queen is prepared to be tolerant. Perhaps even more tolerant than King Henry and our poor cousin were of her religion."

"Tolerant! Of the true religion?" Jane

181

retorted with a flash of her old fire. Then she sagged. "I suppose tolerance is all we can hope for at the moment. God must give us strength to bear this until we can once more change it."

"Jane! Speak not so! Our only hope for your release depends on the peaceful acceptance of her grace's religion and the assurance that the Protestants will not rebel. One sniff of rebellion and you are lost, my lady."

Jane looked at Edward steadily. "And yet, my lord, I would gladly lose this life if I knew that once again the word of God as it is truly interpreted would hold sway over England. I am nothing. God, our heavenly Father, is all. This life here is nothing. It is the life hereafter that will be our reward."

"I know. I too love God, even as you do. But I love you also, my lady, and I do not want you to die. Even if I never see you again, I do not want you to die."

"Edward, my truly beloved, it is even as the scriptures teach us: 'To every thing there is a season . . . a time to be born, and a time to die.' I am not afraid of death, Edward. Nor should you be. Perhaps it will only be in death that we two will finally be reunited . . ."

For a long time after Edward left, Jane sat staring at the reflection of her dying candle in the tiny window. Then she took up her quill and began to write again.

14

... And a time to die

August turned into September. September hurled
itself towards a blazing October. The Duke of
Northumberland, amid great protestations of
faith and repentance for having strayed from the
true path, converted back to Catholicism and
begged to be allowed to attend Mass at the small
chapel of St. Peter ad Vincula on the Tower
Green. Notwithstanding his miraculous recon-
version, he was tried, sentenced and executed,
and his body was laid to rest in the chapel beside
the body of the Duke of Somerset.

The date for Guilford and Jane's trial had not
yet been set. In fact, Mary seemed almost to have
forgotten them. Her coronation was to take place
on the first day of October, and already there
were rumours of a proposed marriage with Philip
of Spain. The rumours, however, were ugly.
Although her reign so far had been tolerant, no
Protestant would accept an alliance with Catholic Spain, and even some Catholics were against
it. Hatred and fear of Spain were too deeply
etched into the fabric of the English nation to
allow them to accept a Spanish king.

For Jane, however, these months were a

peaceful time. She was allowed to have books, she walked in the warm sun, and gradually her health came back to her. Guilford's brothers' wives were allowed to join them in Beauchamp Tower. Occasionally she saw them walking on the leads, but neither they nor Guilford were allowed to communicate with her. Jane was not sorry. Her present serenity had been achieved with pain; it was too fragile to survive a scene with them or with Guilford, who was still alternately distraught and raging, so she was informed.

Only one thing disturbed her. This was the discovery of an unfortunate old and sickly lion that was kept penned in a filthy enclosure near the entrance. It was kept as a curiosity, for the amusement of the nobles who came to tease it now and then. Jane had heard its lonely, frustrated roars, and had demanded to be shown it, but after she had seen it once she could not bring herself to return. Somehow its captivity reminded her only too painfully of her own. She could not avoid hearing it, however, and its roaring disturbed her more than she could bear to admit.

Finally word came that their trial was to be held on November fourteenth, barely a month after Jane's sixteenth birthday. The fine autumn weather had given way to winter by then, and the day dawned cold and blustery. Jane chose her clothes with care. She was dressed in a simple black gown turned back underneath an overskirt of black velvet. On her head she wore a black satin hood with jet trimming. As she left her

184

room, she picked up the small black velvet-bound prayer book that was her daily comfort.

Jane and her two woman attendants were escorted down to the waiting barge, and there, for the first time since their imprisonment, she met Guilford again. He looked thin and tired. He too was dressed in black, in a satin doublet slashed with white. The elegant clothes only seemed to enhance his pallor. Impulsively Jane reached out to hold his hand as they took their places in the barge.

"How goes it with you, my lord?" she asked gently.

"How goes it?" he repeated bitterly. "Marry, how should it go? I am imprisoned, my lady. My father has been murdered, and I am like to follow suit. Think you things should go well with me? I am lost! Ruined!"

"For shame, Lord Guilford. I am sorry for you, of course, for the loss of your father, but you should show more spirit."

Petulantly, Guilford snatched his hand away from hers.

Jane stubbornly retrieved it. "Come, my lord. Let us at least offer each other what poor consolation we may. I am assured that even though we stand trial, we shall be pardoned. You must take heart."

Guilford would not answer, but he left his hand in hers.

In the city they left the barge and walked towards Guildhall. Here Guilford and Jane were separated. Jane walked first, her two gentlewomen behind her. Behind them came Guilford,

Archbishop Cranmer, who was to be tried for heresy, and two of the Dudley brothers, Henry and Ambrose. Four hundred halberdiers lined the street, holding back the crowds of curious onlookers. Jane could not stand the stares, and lowered her eyes to the prayer book which she carried open in front of her.

On entering Guildhall, the prisoners were conducted to the Hall of Justice. Because of her royal blood, Jane was granted the privilege of a chair draped with scarlet cloth and a foot stool. Her women stood beside her. Cranmer was placed in a railed-off pew by himself, separated by a light barrier from the three other men.

Jane looked around her, a tightness gathering in her chest. She was finding it difficult to breathe. Enormous as the vaulted chamber was, there didn't seem to be enough air. She raised her eyes to the dais above her, where sat an assemblage of the nobles of England, including the Chief Justice of the Common Pleas. Then, deepening her distress, Jane saw that the emblems of the Catholic faith, which had been cast out under King Edward, had all been restored. On a small altar stood a crucifix and six golden candlesticks. Even as she stared at these articles of an alien faith, the Lord Mayor's chaplain opened the proceedings with the *Veni, Sancte Spiritus* and other prayers, all in Latin. Jane's heart sank. There could be no justice for her here.

No witnesses were brought forward on either side, nor were the prisoners cross-examined, nor was any defense made. A jury was empanelled and sworn. The charges were read out, the prisoners arraigned to plead guilty or otherwise. Cranmer and the others immediately cried out in loud voices, "Not guilty!" When it came Jane's turn, she could barely find breath enough to speak. In a small, faltering voice, she uttered one word only: "Guilty." How could she plead otherwise? Her only hope lay in Mary's mercy and the possibility of a pardon.

Within twenty minutes the jury returned.

"The sufficient and probable evidence, my lords," their spokesman proclaimed, "is in favour of the queen's grace. We, therefore, return a verdict of guilty."

The Chief Justice stood up. His voice trembled.

"The Lady Jane Dudley is hereby condemned to death — to be burned alive or beheaded, as the queen shall please.

"The Lord Guilford Dudley is hereby condemned to death — to be hanged and quartered at Tyburn.

"His lordship, the Archbishop Cranmer, is hereby condemned to death — to be hanged and quartered at Tyburn.

"The Court in its most gracious mercy extends pardon to the Lords Ambrose and Henry Dudley, recognizing that they merely obeyed their lord father and had no hand in the plotting of heresy or treason."

Jane heard the words with difficulty, as through a mist. Her eyes were fixed on the ceremonial gilded axe of the Royal Guardsman. Upon their entrance he had been holding it normally. But with the pronouncement of the Chief Justice's sentence, he had reversed the blade, so its sharp, pitiless edge now pointed towards the condemned prisoners.

Jane returned to the waiting barge cocooned in shock. She was not aware of the others behind her, or of the sympathetic faces that now lined the streets as the Guard walked before them, the axe reversed. All other feelings in the populace had given way to pity for the slight, solitary figure who walked clutching a small black book in her hands.

The cold river winds touched her not at all as they were taken downriver back to the Tower. No triumphant entrance through the Queen's Gate this time. The rowers shipped their oars as they passed it, then slipped in under the grim, low arch of the Traitors' Gate. The rotten, decaying smell of the moat hit them with full force. No delicate posy to help Jane ward it off today, only rough, disrespectful hands urging her out of the barge and up the dreadful slime-covered steps.

When she reached her lodging, she was greeted by tears and sobs. Mrs. Partridge was wailing, even Mr. Partridge was wiping away tears. Jane's own ladies, who had wept steadily throughout the whole trip, now broke down completely and cried aloud. Jane alone remained dry-eyed. She tried to speak to them, choked, then finally found her voice. "Remember, my beloved friends, that even though I am innocent — even though I did not deserve this sentence — *I should not have accepted the crown.*"

Nothing remained now but to wait and trust in Mary's promise of a pardon.

*　　*　　*

Each day now Mr. Partridge brought disturbing news back to the little house. Mary was determined to go through with her marriage to Philip of Spain. She would not even consider setting Jane and Guilford free until Catholicism was once more firmly established in England and an Anglo-Spanish dynasty founded by her union with Philip. Her actions were causing a rising tide of anti-Catholicism throughout the land. Once more there was talk of rioting and unrest. By Christmas, Jane's daily walks had been curtailed and she was confined to the house.

"But why?" she railed. "What possible threat to her grace am I, shut up here within the Tower?"

"The Protestants are rampaging, my lady. There is talk that they will set you or the Princess Elizabeth up as the head of a Protestant rebellion against the queen." Mr. Partridge looked at Jane fearfully as he relayed this news.

"Am I then to be used against my will again? Do my wishes count for nothing?" Jane raged, but she already knew the answer. "And the Princess Elizabeth, what is she doing?"

"She has retired to her estates, my lady, and has let it be known that she is too ill to leave or to see anyone."

"She is clever," Jane muttered. "She knows how to protect herself. No one will ever trap *her.*"

But there was nothing Jane could do to protect herself. She could only sit by the window in her room and wait.

Shortly after Christmas her wait was ended. There was a knock on her door, and she opened it to see the white, terrified face of Mr. Partridge.

"Sir Thomas Wyatt has roused the people against the queen, my lady. He has an enormous force and is gathering more and more to his cause each day. He is marching on London to remove the queen from the throne!"

"And with whom does he intend to replace her?" Jane asked. A terrible coldness was settling around her heart.

"With the Princess Elizabeth, they say. But —"

"But what?"

"But —" Partridge seemed unable to go on. When he did continue, his voice had sunk till it was almost inaudible. "But your lord father has joined with him, my lady, and there are those who say he means to put you back on the throne."

The fire crackled on in the silence. The winter rains streamed down the windowpanes. In the distance, the lion roared forlornly.

Sir Thomas advanced quickly upon London. The city made ready to defend itself. Finally the news came that he was in Southwark, right across the river from the Tower, and the city was besieged. The citizens of London ran to and fro in a frenzy. The noise of their screaming and the hammering as houses and shops were hastily boarded up could be heard even in the Tower.

"The queen refuses to leave the city and seek safety," Mr. Partridge reported, admiration in his voice. "She is at Guildhall herself, overseeing the preparations and supplies!"

The ordinances and cannon of the Tower were trained upon the shores of Southwark, an easy distance away, but Mary refused to give the order for them to fire.

"Her grace will not risk the lives of the innocent people of Southwark, no matter how threatened she is," Mr. Partridge added breathlessly.

The drawbridge of London Bridge remained raised, however, and try as he might, Sir Thomas Wyatt could not cross the river under the threatening guns of the Tower. There would be no compunction about firing at him on the water.

In desperation, the rebel forces retreated and attempted an attack from the west. They repaired to Kingston and managed to cross the river there, then marched on Charing Cross.

Inside the Tower everything was confusion. The leads were lined with frightened noblemen and their ladies who had taken refuge in the Tower, all staring anxiously towards the west, trying to make out what was happening. The noise of battle drifted back to them, mingled with screams, shouts and cries. The city was in chaos.

Jane shut her door, closed her window, and knelt by her bed to pray. Her mind echoed the confusion reigning through the Tower and the city outside her room. How could she not pray for release? And yet, could she pray for release at such a price? Screams. The noise of battle. Her closed window did not shut out the sound of the bloodshed that was coming closer and closer.

And then there was silence. Not suddenly, not even noticeably at first, but gradually the guns ceased, the screams and cries became fewer and fewer.

"Shall I go and find out what has happened?" Mrs. Ellen asked tremulously, rising from knees that were cramped with hours of kneeling.

Jane put out her hand to stop her. "No, stay. We shall know soon enough."

Not long after, Mr. Partridge stumbled up the stairs to bring them the news. Sir Thomas Wyatt had been beaten and had surrendered. The Duke of Suffolk had been taken prisoner.

Now Jane knew what to pray for.

"Thou knowest, oh God, better what is good for me than I do. Do with me in all things what Thou wilt, and plague me what way Thou wilt. Only" — the remembrance of the sharp, cutting edge of the axe turned towards her was suddenly very vivid, and her voice faltered — "only, in the meantime, arm me, I beseech Thee, with Thy armour, that I may stand fast . . ." Her head dropped into her hands and the bitter tears fell scalding through her fingers.

* * *

Through the mercy of Queen Mary, Jane's sentence was commuted from burning to beheading. Guilford, also, was to be spared the agony of being hung, then drawn and quartered while still alive. He too would be beheaded. Jane, because she was of royal blood, would be executed in the relative privacy of Tower Green, but Guilford would die on Tower Hill, in public. Mary graciously granted the husband and wife the privilege of one last meeting, but Jane refused.

"Will you not see him, my lady? He has requested it most piteously." Mrs. Partridge wrung her hands and twisted the apron she wore almost into shreds.

"Does he weep still?"

"Yes, my lady."

"Send word to him that I will pray for him. That he must be brave and pray to God. I will watch for him as he goes. Thanks to the mercy of our queen, the pain will be brief." She paused for a moment, then continued. "The time is short now. We must both prepare ourselves."

Jane set about preparing herself with scrupulous thoroughness. In these last few hours her papers and most of her books had been taken from her, but she still had her Greek Testament, her prayer book, and writing materials. The Greek Testament would go to Katherine. In it she wrote:

I have here sent you, my dear sister Katherine, a book, which although it be not outwardly trimmed with gold, or the curious embroidery of the artfullest needles, yet inwardly it is more worth than all the precious mines which the vast world can boast of: it is the book, beloved sister, of the Law of the Lord . . .

Her quill scratched in the silence as she wrote.

Then she turned to her little black velvet-bound prayer book. She would send that to her father, to comfort him in his own imprisonment. Perhaps he would once again squirm his way free? She doubted it. For all he was to blame, he

193

would need solace as much as she now. She thought for a while, then penned a message to him in the narrow margins of the book:

The Lord comfort your grace . . .

The words came haltingly at first, then more easily. Sir John Bridges, the Lieutenant of the Tower, who had been kind to her, would give it to him.

Now all that remained was to compose and memorize the last words she would speak at her execution. This was the most difficult task of all — it was important to die well.

The following morning Jane rose early and dressed carefully in the same simple black gown and overskirt she had worn to her trial. She placed the Greek testament with her last message to Katherine on her writing table, to be picked up and sent on to her sister later by Mrs. Partridge. Her prayer book she held tightly in her hands. She would keep it with her until the last minute and give it to Sir John Bridges when
—

Not allowing herself to finish the thought, she walked slowly to the window overlooking the Tower Green and stationed herself there. Guilford would be brought by soon on his way to Tower Hill. She had promised she would watch for him.

*   *   *

. . . The small procession appeared, Guilford walking in the middle. His face was white, but Jane saw with pride that he was not weeping, and he held his head high. She watched until the procession moved out of her view. Still she waited. Barely half an hour later she heard the rumble of cart wheels. The same procession — but Guilford no longer walked with them. Jane forced herself to look at the poor, bloodstained body lying within the cart.

"Guilford, Guilford . . ." She was not aware that she was speaking. Her mind was praying. For her husband. For herself. Guilford's trial was over. Hers was now to come.

The knock on her door came soon after. Mrs. Ellen and Elizabeth Tylney were huddled together in one corner of the room, weeping so desperately they couldn't answer it. Jane walked over and opened the door herself. Sir John Bridges stood on the threshold. Silently he offered her his arm, and she placed her hand upon it. In her other hand she held the prayer book.

"Come, my ladies," she said softly to the two weeping women. "Will you not assist me?"

Clutching onto each other for support, they followed.

Sir John led her out of the house and across the Green to the scaffold. It seemed to Jane that it took an eternity for them to mount the few steps up to where the towering scarlet-clad figure of the headsman waited. When they reached the top, Sir John dropped her hand and stepped aside. Jane turned away from her executioner and faced the gathering that peered up at her. Now was the time she must recite the few words she had rehearsed the night before. She took a deep breath.

"Good people, I am come hither to die." Her voice rang out clear and true. "By law I am condemned to the same. The fact, indeed, against the Queen's Highness was unlawful, and the consenting thereunto by me. But it was never my seeking, but by counsel of those who should seem to have further understanding of these things than I, who knew little of the law, and much less of the titles to the Crown.

"I pray you all, good Christian people, to bear me witness that I die a true Christian woman, and that I look to be saved by the mercy of God —" For the first time her voice faltered, but she recovered and went on.

"And now, good people, while I am alive, I pray you to assist me with your prayers."

Queen Mary's own chaplain stepped forward to help her as she kneeled and in a quiet, steady voice, recited the fifty-first Psalm. Then she rose to her feet again. For five minutes Jane stood there, in total silence, according to the law, waiting for the possibility of a reprieve. It did not come.

At the end of the allotted time, Sir John Bridges touched her lightly on the elbow. She turned to him and silently handed him the prayer book. She took off her gloves. She was pleased to see that her hands were trembling only slightly as she gave the gloves to Elizabeth Tylney. She began to untie the upper part of her gown. Mrs.

Ellen moved to help her, but the old lady's body sagged and she collapsed, sobbing uncontrollably. The executioner stepped forward as if he would assist her, but Jane shrank back.

"Let me alone," she commanded. She had forgotten that the garment was his by right to take as his fee.

Elizabeth Tylney finally helped her to remove it, baring her neck and shoulders, but when it came to performing the final duty for her mistress — that of blindfolding her with the fine handkerchief Jane had chosen the night before — she too gave way. Jane was left holding it herself.

The executioner approached again, then knelt. "Do you forgive me, madam?"

This time Jane remembered the ritual. She looked down at him quietly. "Most willingly," she replied.

He stood up, and finally Jane looked beyond him to the block. She felt her body begin to shake in spite of herself.

"Stand upon the straw, madam."

Jane stepped forward, her eyes riveted on the cold stone.

"I pray you, dispatch me quickly," she whispered. With her own hands she tied the handkerchief around her eyes, willing with a desperate intensity that her fingers should not fumble. She knelt and reached out for the block. It was not there. In the darkness she was suddenly alone and terrified.

"Where is it?" she cried. "Where is it?"

There was no reply. Only silence.

What shall I do?

Then, from out of the darkness, she felt a hand on her shoulder, gently guiding her forward. She reached out and her fingers closed almost thankfully on the hard, roughened surface. She felt for the curved aperture where she must place her head, paused, then laid her cheek against the stone. She closed her eyes. Only a few second more . . .

"Lord, into Thy hands I commend my spirit!" With a sudden move, Jane threw out her arms.

The headsman knew the signal. He raised his axe. The blade glistened briefly in the pale, wintry sunlight, then flashed down once in a final, shining arc.

Epilogue

Jane's father, the Duke of Suffolk, was executed on Tower Hill on February 24, 1554. Her mother, the Duchess, retained the favour and friendship of Queen Mary, and was soon remarried to Adrian Stokes, a man much younger than she. This caused a great scandal at court.

Katherine's marriage to Lord Herbert was annulled upon the accession of Queen Mary. Eight years later she secretly married Edward Seymour, Earl of Hertford. Elizabeth I, who had become queen after Mary's death in 1558, was furious about this marriage. She was aware that the two remaining Grey sisters were possible rivals for the succession, and did not want to see them establishing families. Elizabeth had Katherine and Edward imprisoned in the Tower, with strict orders that they were not to see each other. Nevertheless, they had two sons, the older of whom is an ancestor of Queen Elizabeth II.

Jane's youngest sister, Mary, married Thomas Keyes, Sergeant Porter at Court. Queen Elizabeth was equally angry about this marriage, and put Mary into custody in a succession of country houses. Eventually, after her husband was dead, she was allowed to go and live with her stepfather and his wife, her mother having by then died.

Jane's body remained unattended on the scaffold for most of the rest of the day while officials wrangled over what should be done with it. Because she was a Protestant, they refused to allow her burial in the now once again Catholic St. Peter ad Vincula. Eventually, however, permission was obtained, and there, alongside Henry's two equally unfortunate queens, Anne Boleyn and Catherine Howard, she was finally laid to rest.